THE RED HOG
OF COLIMA

THE RED HOG OF COLIMA

Scottish Short Stories
1989

Preface by John Linklater

COLLINS
8 Grafton Street, London W1
1989

William Collins Sons & Co. Ltd
London · Glasgow · Sydney · Auckland
Toronto · Johannesburg

First published 1989
The Red Hog of Colima © Erik Coutts; *The Fly* © Peter Regent; *Saints' Holiday* © John Kerr; *The Lotus-Blossom Jesus* © Chris Arthur; *Survivors* © Susan Chaney; *Brain Cancer* © Jenny Turner; *Spring Morning with Alp* © Drummond Bone; *From a Moth-Eaten Ethnographical Manuscript* © Frank Kuppner; *The Poster* © Ken Ross; *Heroes* © Carole Morin; *The Miracle of Jonah* © William Raeper; *The Sighting* © Moira Burgess; *The Wall* © Justine Cable; *Warmth* © Tim Niel; *Best Friends* © Jennifer Murray; *The Fox's Nest* © John Cunningham, originally printed in *Panurge 8*; *The Face* © Brian McCabe.

The Publisher acknowledges the financial assistance of the Scottish Arts Council in the publication of this volume.

BRITISH LIBRARY CATALOGUING IN PUBLICATION DATA

The Red Hog of Colima
1. Short stories in English.
Scottish writers, 1989. Anthologies
823'.01'089411 [FS]

ISBN 0-00-223549-8 (pbk)
ISBN 0-00-223548 X (h/b)

Photoset in Linotron Imprint by
Rowland Phototypesetting Limited, Bury St Edmunds.
Printed and Bound in Great Britain by
William Collins Sons & Co. Ltd, Glasgow

CONTENTS

Preface by John Linklater	7
Erik Coutts THE RED HOG OF COLIMA	11
Peter Regent THE FLY	19
John Kerr SAINTS' HOLIDAY	37
Chris Arthur THE LOTUS-BLOSSOM JESUS	49
Susan Chaney SURVIVORS	55
Jenny Turner BRAIN CANCER	65
Drummond Bone SPRING MORNING WITH ALP	79
Frank Kuppner FROM A MOTH-EATEN ETHNOGRAPHICAL MANUSCRIPT	87
Ken Ross THE POSTER	93
Carole Morin HEROES	99
William Raeper THE MIRACLE OF JONAH	107

CONTENTS

Moira Burgess   117
THE SIGHTING

Justine Cable   123
THE WALL

Tim Niel   135
WARMTH

Jennifer Murray   151
BEST FRIENDS

John Cunningham   159
THE FOX'S NEST

Brian McCabe   181
THE FACE

Biographical Notes   187

PREFACE

FIRST, a confession.
Eight years ago an earlier volume in this annual short story series struck me as so poor, so lacking in quality writing or editorial adventure, that it served no useful purpose. A review of *Scottish Short Stories 1981* appeared above my name in the *Glasgow Herald* and now seems consumed with its own vitriol. It applied the term 'unworthy' to the majority of the eighteen contributions appearing in that volume, making the cheap jibe that the book's dustjacket design, an elegant one which was retained for several years, lent a dignity to the authors, 'few of their literary efforts deserve'. The purist tone of that review was highly unattractive, but I still hold by the view that, with the two exceptions I made at the time, it was a weak collection, illustrative of the folly of playing safe.

But my criticism was not only malicious, it was largely misdirected. When I disputed that the purpose of the volume could possibly be seen as encouraging young talent, it was on the ludicrous grounds that no included author was under the age of thirty. When I denied that it could be regarded as an 'annual showcase' for Scottish writing, it was on the contradictory grounds that there were too many established writers, and that more should be expected from them. Given the fragile rewards and securities which attend professional writing today in this part of the world, I am no longer sure that the term 'established Scottish writer' has any meaning. Eight years ago I suspect I would have defined 'established' as ripe for abuse. Fortunately, not all of my personalized attacks on individual writers appeared in print. The piece was edited for legal reasons, I recall. Just as well. I'd missed the point there too.

No writer should be blamed for delving deep into a bottom drawer to retrieve some overlooked piece, perhaps some previously rejected or discarded piece, for the purpose of making a submission. Such a circumstance might apply only in rare instances. After all, there is more integrity among writers than in most other walks of life. Their job requires integrity. Good writing is an expression of integrity. But, I suggest, if such a circumstance should apply and a bottom-drawer story is submitted, it is not the writer who should be blamed. Blame the editor who accepts it. Blame the editor, particularly if acceptance is with a view to ornamenting a collection with names of repute, rather than stories of substance. Or stories to disturb the peace, to quote Archie Hind's commendable object in *Dear Green Place*.

Happily, substance and repute are by no means mutually exclusive, as a number of recognized writers have demonstrated eloquently in their valued contributions to this series over the years. The fact that this year's editors (Dorothy Porter, JoAnne Robertson and myself) have settled for a selection among which there are relatively few 'established' writers is entirely coincidental. We have subscribed to a trend which has been growing in recent volumes. It is precisely this trend which encouraged me to agree readily to join the panel of editors who considered the short story submissions for this year. Therefore, permit me to endorse the observation of one reviewer of last year's collection, *I Can Sing, Dance, Rollerskate*, the first in this series to require a reprint, that there seemed to be fewer well-established writers and more new ones. This estimable reviewer, Isobel Murray in the *Scotsman*, added: 'the general effect is that a lot of new talent is coming upon us, and it is exhilarating'. Perhaps her position, and mine in 1981, are not so divorced. Hers, however, is phrased a little more felicitously.

But there is a more fundamental reason why reputations were irrelevant to our selections for this year's volume. In

PREFACE

advance of any stories being submitted, the decision was taken that they should be passed to the editors without the names of their authors. I am certain that our consideration of stories entirely on their own merits was no more pronounced than among previous panels of editors. We simply made it easier for ourselves to operate in this fashion. Even so, there are Scottish writers whose signatures are etched deeply into ever phrase they write, and we could hardly fail to recognize a few. Neither could we fail to recognize that in other stories new voices were speaking. That did not trouble us, because some of those fresh and young voices spoke urgently, and it was not difficult for us to ensure that they would be heard here.

Only after we had made our final selection were we given the names of the authors. When, as it were, we learned what we had done, it was with some relief that we considered our red hog in a poke. It offers reasonable continuity with its immediate predecessor volumes. Like Deirdre Chapman, in her preface three years ago, we can claim, 'This is a very democratic volume,' because we have arranged new writers alongside others who have gained, or who are gaining, recognition. In our self-inflicted blindness we have not overlooked Moira Burgess, Frank Kuppner, Brian McCabe and Peter Regent, who have appeared in previous volumes and are here represented again. Ken Ross has returned for a second successive year, and quite rightly. He is a coming force. Of the three (at least) writers whose appearance here marks the publication of their first short stories the youngest is twenty-four. And they are all women. We welcome Susan Chaney, Jennifer Murray and Jenny Turner.

We offer them, and the rest of our thirteen authors, as our reply to the argument made recently by Douglas Dunn, a welcome contributor to previous volumes in this series and a Scottish writer of deserved international reputation, that editors of this collection should commission rather than select. We have continued to select, and by our selections we hope to have facilitated stories that are good, writers who are going to become good, and writing that is fresh and stimulating. Commissioning editors are drawn to contributors who are perceived to be reliably good, or who will attract attention. There is a place for such an approach to a volume of Scottish short stories, but it is not the one envisaged for this series when it was launched in 1973.

Nevertheless, we *have* commissioned. Following on from last year, it is the intention of the publishers and the Scottish Arts Council to seek jacket illustrations for this and future volumes from young Scottish artists. We thank Alison Watt, whose *Renfrewshire Pig* has helped deliver this red hog of a book to you, its readers. We hope you enjoy it.

JOHN LINKLATER
Glasgow, December 1988

THE RED HOG OF COLIMA

Erik Coutts

We have few sayings. Only one is known to all of us. In their need, the old retain the others. But one we know. I am poor, therefore I hate. And despite the priest, we feel this to be true. For what else does a man possess? A woman? A patch of corn, many children? Yes, these. But every Indian has these things, and the Mestizos too, yet every living man is poor.

My woman says that a poor man lies down too easily. She is fond of telling me this. For her sympathy has died. Daily, her voice is growing harder. (Can there be another sound like this?) Her voice is changed. There is no laughter now, she is sore all the time. And she calls me a *bum*. And this pains me. It is unjust.

Did I not tend the chairs at Manzanillo for three summers? And groom my hair in the brilliantine? Did I not learn of the gringo ways before any in our village? I doffed my hat when the gringos stepped off their beautiful launches. I smiled, I bowed, I was heavy with courtesies. And I sold them the mixture of pine needles and ginger that they might breathe. Only I could speak of the blue hair of their women. And those fingernails held out like almonds. I knew them all. I was their friend. 'Bo-hoy' they called me. This was their word for me, and I was their friend, I was Bo-hoy. And I tended the chairs – even at noon – receiving many centavos for each chair. Are *these* the achievements of a bum? Who before me knew of showers, and how the water comes with force? Or how the gringos cover their mouths with tape before they use these showers? I would call myself many things before I called myself a bum.

And yet I am poor. Since we boiled the rooster, I am some way worse than poor – I am alone and weary with my hatred. Why *me*? I ask the priest – of all the men in this village, why am I so solitary poor? My son, that is simple, says the priest – this matter concerns what we term the verities – plainly, you have yet to discover God – when your heart is pure, then you will be rich. This, the priest tells me. And he's a wise fellow. He understands the workings of a man's soul. He knows the verities and I respect him. I respect his age and his many recoveries from an old man's agony. But now I cannot believe his words, for if it is my soul that waits to become pure – why should my children's bellies hurt in the meantime? Of course, I do not say these things to the priest, but I ask my woman – later, at the well – and she says, 'Because they are doomed, they are of seed that is bad. Their father is a bum.'

And again she tells me of the time her father sold his burros. In Jalisco. Before the time of the Pepsi plant. Woman, I say – this story pains me as no other. But she tells it nonetheless, and fiercely she grips her hair that I might feel the pain in *my* hair: Her father took his burros into Jalisco. In '41, when the ash came. And I followed thirty strides behind, for I was his newest son-in-law. I carried the cooking pot, and the pouch of beans, and the machete, and many other things besides. Often the old man would stop for tequila. And when he drank, I would round up the burros for they were a straying kind. (Always these creatures can smell the shed snakeskins on a trail, and that puts unease in their blood. The burro lives with the smell of rattlesnakes. And pumas. It is his way.)

And so we forded the Armería and went into Jalisco. There we met a man who offered thirty pesos for the burros. My father-in-law was heavy with tequila then, and with scorn too, and he said, 'Do you think we are so stupid in Colima? Always the traders of Jalisco are rogues! These animals are worth sixty pesos – and two cans of purified oil besides.' And he fell into bargaining with this rogue and sent me away that I might not weaken the power in his voice.

In the village I met an Otomi – I speak their language well-enough. And he was a sly one, like all his people, and I held the bean pouch close to me. He belonged to a village beyond the Balano, a place where the air was good and children did not fall before the fever. He visited his home on feast days and at the time of the corn harvest. The rest of the time he worked for a coffee grower named Núñez, a good employer who beat him only the once in every month and who provided him with a fine dwelling and an extra hammock for visitors. To prove this, he showed me the hammock, and I lay in it, and smoked his leaf, and listened to the story of the red hog.

Núñez had paid six hundred for him. Naturally, he cherished this hog more than a woman. It weighed as much as three men and lived on mounds of corn and beans, and it *glowed* in the first sun of the day. A man was paid to watch over it whilst it ate, and in this way no one stole the creature's food. Another rubbed oil into its hide, or made a wallow for it with many pails of water carried from the spring. Throughout Jalisco the hog was famous and all who worked for Núñez would hang around the pen so they might witness the sun in its coat. And, of course, these men wanted the hog for their own, to cherish it in the first sun and watch it in the full pride of their leisure.

'Show me this animal!' I said. 'Show it to me and I will believe this thing, for to us of Colima the Otomi are a byword for dishonesty.' At this, the man smiled in his slow, Otomi style. 'Two pesos is the price,' he said. 'Such an animal deserves such a sum.' I told him I had no more than one peso in my shoe, but should I send my spit further than his, I would give him the peso and he would show me the great hog. Otherwise, he could keep his money and I would not trouble him again.

'I agree,' said the Otomi at once, for as well as liars that race are redoubtable spitters and he found me a betel nut beneath his mattress and asked that I chew on it so each might know the other's mark – for his part, he would use red clay. I chewed. Then I sent a fine brown spit down the track. The Otomi also, and with much power in his teeth. And we checked the marks, and he agreed I was a truly great spitter, *far* removed from being a bum, and he took my peso and led me through the trees to the pen of the red hog. When I saw the creature, I wanted him for my own! I will say this: in all my life I had *never* seen such a fine thing – and I do not forget the railway tracks at Uruápan. For the sun shone in his coat like an August dawn! Truly, I was moved. And I watched him in his wallow, digging like a king, and the day went down like a sigh and still I watched, and in the dusk I listened to his fine snores.

Within the dosshouse of Ramon Casafuerte, my father-in-law rolled in sleep. From his ears the wax had started to show, for such is the effect of tequila on the very old. I drew close to him. My body was shaking but I thought of the hog and became at ease. Then I removed the old man's sandal, and opened the sole with my switchblade: many pesos – in the paper style, with the face of the hero and the ocote pine tree – and these I took and stuffed within my blouse, and breathed again, and went out into the night: to the shack of the Otomi. 'Here are *many* pesos,' I said to his new face. 'More than you will see in all your life, more than an Otomi village will ever behold. Help me drive the red hog to the scar of the hill, to the place that does not smell of ash, and all these will be yours.' At once, the Otomi knew vexation, and he said, 'I'll be discovered – for as you well know, that is the way of an Otomi – it is his destiny to be discovered and find refuge only in the grave. For stealing the red hog, I will be flogged, or killed – and certainly you will be killed.' At this, he looked to his feet, and waited that I should admit I was a fool, that I should return to the dosshouse and leave him to the deeper stages of the night. Naturally, I did not admit these things. Never are the men of Colima more serious than when greed plays in their nostrils. Besides, I burned with need for the red hog. And presently, the Otomi understood, and for a long time he shook his head and rocked, which is typical of that people when they are thinking. Then he rose – and gave me mescal – and when we finished we said nothing but went on light feet to the wallow.

The red king slept, and his back rose out of the wallow and touched the moon. To the Otomi, this was a good omen, though I had not heard of it until then. We opened the sisal fence with our blades. And the hog came out of his sleep at once, as a hog will, and he looked at us with his serious eyes. 'Uffuffuffuffuffuff,' I said to him. 'Do not be afraid old fellow, for now you are coming to Colima with me.' And I came close to him and patted the dust and the night from his coat, and truly my hand was a child's hand on the archway of his back! Then I guess he smelled the Otomi and took fright, for he ran twice around his yard with a sound in his chest such as a young dog makes when he is learning to bark. 'Let's get out've here!' said the Otomi, and he looked up at the moon which now stood on Colima's cone and in his eyes there was doubt.

But the red hog was wise, even in his fear, for he stopped and panted, and found himself at the hole we had cut, and went calmly through as a priest might when he leaves the house of a dead man. Then we followed him, and in our hearts we were as free as any dead man. My pig took no driving and we ran behind him all the way to the scar on the hill.

'Now I must go,' the Otomi said. 'I have seen this deal to this point and that is its end – you can smell for yourself how the ash has gone out of the air – now I'll take my money.' And I gave him the money, but my haunches trembled, and I said, 'Suppose a puma comes out of the night and kills my hog! Or he falls in quicksand and my strength cannot move him. Stay with me on the trail, until the first sun settles on his coat, no longer I promise.' But the sly one shook his head, saying, 'If a puma takes him, I would not wish to be near you or your animal. And if he falls in quicksand I could not pull on him for my shoulder is inflamed from a knife wound. So adiós. May your hog tell no tales.' This angered me, you realize. 'You sonofabitch!' I shouted. 'You undescended Otomi!' And I threw a rock after him, but it landed only in the mesquite, for in that darkness there was no sound of pain.

Down the trail the hog had paused that his great loins might cool. I approached him with much veneration. We were in the clean air and we felt good. On his snout there were many beads of healthy dew. 'Soon you'll be in Colima,' I told him, 'and there will be a great sufficiency of corn, and I will hide you so that none will know of your wallow save I. And I will come often to drive away your loneliness.' This, the red hog understood, and he smelled at the clean air that he might believe me.

On the trail I fed him all the beans I carried. And he was easy to drive. A hog likes to stroll, and he could smell the coast and wanted to be there. It cost me the machete to cross the Armería and when the ferryman put us down the air was black as never before.

When the cone of Colima broke its fire it was hard to breathe. The moon smoked and was lost. And about us there was a wind. The sky was running before the ash. I thought of my father-in-law, for he was back there in the wind itself. And I watched the fire in that wind and the trails of red that went through the night. Truly, this was a terrible thing. The sky of Jalisco was burning about the rim of the darkness and I led my hog into air that was unspoiled and presently to a place where I could breathe my guilt.

I made a pen. It was enough. Water ran close by. The hog was content. But he was also leaner now and his feet were red-sore. But none should find him there, and of this I was sure. And for two days, I too laid low. Then I went to my woman and told her the lies. There was much mourning. Many people had died beneath the mountain of Colima, but my woman only had the one father and this she told me, so many times.

Then there was the rain, more than I had ever witnessed, and always from the black heart of that sky. I did not see the coat of the red hog glow. The sky was held in darkness.

THE RED HOG OF COLIMA

But I spoke to my animal with much love and brought him cobs, the last we had, and wooden boards that his roof might not leak.

When the cobs were gone, I fell again to stealing. All the soldiers had gone into Jalisco for there were great fires still. And it was simple to remove gringo sorghum from the granary of the Miramon family – and I was not guilty in such theft for they were a hated race in those days and tainted by their deeds.

But my woman had fallen ill. And her milk was harmful and our child wasted. The priest shook his head – God's disfavour is in the blackness of that sky, he said. And he made us pray. But when we had prayed, we fell quiet in fear. The old women talked of the four dead woodpeckers and how the buzzards had left them untouched, and went instead into the deeper blackness in the east. 'There is evil in this place,' the old women said. And they lit candles.

Each night, I went to my hog. He was lame – the trail, the rains. 'Eat the gringo sorghum old fellow,' I said, 'eat and retain your hold here, for the rain will cease and then the sun will turn your coat to copper fire!' But he did not eat. He pined, like my child. And he would not touch the sorghum, for at that time I did not realize that this grain is distasteful to the finer animals. And I worried. And when I was not by him I was with my woman, watching over her in the usual way where it is better *not to move*, even the jaw muscles, and I watched and worried here too. And I gave our child to the old women that the redness might go from its belly. And my child died the following day, and we buried it in the ash, in the driest place.

When my woman found strength in the fullness of her fever, we knew she would survive. There were many herbs. I relaxed. 'Woman,' I said, 'our child has perished from the bad milk of your breast, and I have buried her near my family grave where it is dry. But now you will be well and bear further children, and realize that these are the pains and the burdens of all Colima Indians.' And she fell into a grief and a rage such as I could not bear. I went to the pen of the hog to be away from her for a time – through the black rain. And there I found my prize spraddled in the mud, his great limbs fast in the mud.

I watched the last life run out of him – out of his eyes. He sighed. That was his going. And in that warm rain which was black with ash, I stood awhile. Then I tried to drag him to a place where it was dry, that I might make a fire and a fitting end to him. But his weight was great and he would not move.

I watched over him, as I had my woman. Then, in the morning, I went to my house, and the sun appeared, the first in over a week. This, the old women said, was a response to their prayers, to their many candles. The air too – for that was clean and deep as Jalisco where the cone of Colima stood quietly once more. But I thought of the red hog, and the buzzards who would break him on their beaks, and the coat which should not glow in this new sun. And I took our last kerosene and started back. But when I stepped out – there at the well – I met my father-in-law. His eyes were scalded. His clothing too. And (for so I learned when I stopped running and returned in the evening) his voice had burned away also, burned away for good in the fires of Colima. When he looked on me, he spoke only with his eyes. And in time, all in our village knew his message, knew the word he retained for me. Which *pains* me.

THE FLY
Peter Regent

It was wonderful when the fly came. In the cell there was no night or day; only a steady continuum of light. There were punctuations when food arrived, with a bleep and the little lamp flashing at the automatic hatch, but he was sure the hours of delivery were not precisely regular. Apart from that, and the whispering of the microphones, nothing happened. Nothing at all. Then the fly came, and it was wonderful.

It arrived with a shocking, zooming buzz, and a soft, blundering kiss to his deliciously affronted cheek. It buzzed, and that was marvellous too – a suddenly remembered sound, mocking this automated place with the way its mechanical-seeming drone was broken by stops and starts, comings and goings and changes of pitch. But if it was not mechanical, it was not arbitrary either. It was unpredictable because it was wilful; it knew pleasure and pain, had preferences, and it buzzed when it chose! If he became furious and struck at it, it declined to be caught, although – and this was yet another marvel – it might not have so chosen. Or again, it might have done, and then failed to dodge. It was not only wilful, it was also, at least potentially, fallible.

It was even unpleasant, fussing around him when he did not want it, and hiding away when he longed to see it. It would drive him insane with its persistence, then sit inviting death from a smack. It was evocative of all the flies that had hovered over all the markets of the past, because, of course, markets were only in the past; they had been no more than the source of quaint figures of speech for scores of years. It was the same with dungheaps. When, in these days of hygenic recycling, was there last a dungheap in the world? But the fly evoked the idea of markets and dungheaps all the same. It had a will of its own. It was an autonomous, living creature.

What was even more extraordinary was that it had arrived here, in this cell. It should have been impossible for it to penetrate the air filters and the sterilization system. But it had come – his fly; the classic companion and comfort of solitary prisoners throughout the ages. It was beautiful to think of the fly surmounting every modern obstacle to perform its traditional function in this most untraditional of places.

For prisons were no longer what they used to be. After the 'salutary cuts' of 2029, things had never been the same again. Prisons used to involve cruelty, directly by wardens or indirectly by a regime of tolerated bullying by gangster-inmates. There had been systematic exploitation, and there had been cruelty through neglect, or through delegating the disgusting job of custodianship to profit-making agencies. Like so many other things, it had all happened after the coming to power of the In-work Oligarchy. Rocketing labour-costs, coupled with the impossibility of integrating prisoners into any productive process except through slave factories or domestic service (both of them spheres reserved to robots) – were at the root of the problem. As every schoolboy and schoolgirl knows, the answer was found in the automated prison: hygenic and human, educational and economical, and quite, quite, impersonal.

He had not seen anyone for – but of course, there was no way of knowing how long. Like everything else, and axiomatically, it was his own fault. The severity of his offence, and its connection with 'security', had meant he could be allowed no contact with other prisoners. He knew too much. He had made matters worse by his non-cooperation.

He had regarded 'solitary' rather as a challenge, and had

quite enjoyed resisting re-education. He had sat with his back to the wall video, and he had peed into the loudspeaker slots (he was rather proud of that one, since it needed a degree of stoicism to accept the inevitable electric shock). Such things, and reciting poetry to drown the whisper-pillow, had kept his mind occupied. He had broken or smeared so many video windows that the system seemed to have given up trying to reform him. Could it be that the machine was tiring first?

Now he was in an unbreakable cell. He couldn't get at the speakers, and there was no screen to muck up. There must still be the white sound, but he supposed he had become proof against it, for he no longer noticed either that, or the murmurings and whisperings of the re-education programme. He believed he slept a lot, but how could he be sure, with no means of telling the passage of time? He had no idea how long he had been in here.

He fed the fly, and studied it as it ate. Its body was green-black, shiny and metallic, but also hairy, when you looked really close. It had a sort of chip out of one wing; a hereditary defect, perhaps, because the edges were quite smooth. Its bulbous, multiple eyes seemed lit by a dull red glow from inside. Of course, you couldn't tell what it was looking at, because it was looking at everything all the time. Did it attend to all those images at once, then? Its buzzing seemed even less mechanical now he was attuned to its nuances. Dancing its scribbling aerial dance, it seemed in some sort of conversation with itself. Then, when it suddenly zoomed in and hovered round his head, it could be quite heavily confidential – intimate, even – buzzing in his ear and making him squirm with horrid pleasure.

It was a tease. It tested the cracks round the door, but they were too narrow for it. It hung about the ventilation slots, but there was a mesh behind them, thank God. So how had it got here? Might he wake up and find it had gone by the same route? He tried to train it to come for food, and sometimes he thought it responded. But then, it would, wouldn't it?

Sometimes he lay awake worrying lest the fly might die.

It had seemed for some time – how long, there was of course no means of knowing – that meals were being delivered more irregularly and at generally greater intervals. Once or twice he became quite hungry. He waited impatiently for the 'bleep' and the little light by the hatch, then seized the plastic tray when it finally arrived, and fell on the food, even though it was hardly warmed though. More than once he had the impression that the lavatory flushed only grudgingly, and at times the heating was clearly off. Then the ventilation became intermittent, and eventually something quite extraordinary happened – the lights went off. They came on again almost at once, but the shock of darkness after years – yes, it must be years – of continuous light was terrifying. After that first time, the lights flickered often. Then they went out again, and stayed off quite a long while. Soon it was happening so often that he became used to it and began to look forward to the next swallowing-up into velvety darkness. All the same, it was disturbing that things could no longer be relied on. It made one wonder what was going on outside, if there still was an outside.

Then, with a hiss and a sudden draught of air, the door of the cell swung open. He sat gaping at the gap it left, and at the unfamiliar wall, so far away on the other side of the yard-wide corridor. He might have sat in amazement even longer but, with an enthusiastic buzz that faded rapidly into the distance, the fly went out. He leaped up, calling it back. Then he saw the corridor stretching away into vast distance – yard after yard after yard – and felt dizzy. He pulled himself together, and cautiously crept down the passage, following the way the fly must have boldly gone before.

At the end of the corridor was another, at right angles, and at the end of that was a lift. The controls showed several floors ascending to 'Ground'. He pressed 'Ground', and the lift hummed and shook a little, as if considering whether or not to work. Eventually it rose, with grunts and hesitations, and more slowly than he remembered lifts doing. The door opened wheezily on to another corridor, which led to a little office, smelling vaguely unpleasant. There was a computer console, with a screen that was showing the heading 'State of unit S1'. The keyboard was standard. He pressed 'Show' and a series of numbers and names appeared. One name was flashing on and off. It was his, and next to it was the word 'released'.

'Oh my God!'

The archaism seemed necessary to express his confusion. He understood, of course, that his release must have been ordained by the computer, according to some complex formula that scrupulously took account of all his misdemeanours. It was not surprising that the door should open automatically on the appropriate day. Things happened like that, here. But surely there should have been someone to receive him, or at least some instructions for him on the screens at the ends of the corridors?

Still pondering, he turned to go, and saw a heap of rags and rubbish on the floor. He stirred it with his foot, and yelled when a desiccated hand broke through the cloth, and the stale smell he had noticed before suddenly came on more strongly. He blundered out, and ran down corridor after corridor, looking for a way of escape, but finding only two more dried-out corpses. The lights went out again. He groped in the dark, and thought he could hear dull thumping, as if someone was banging on a door somewhere far below; another prisoner, perhaps, sensing that the machine was breaking down, and fearing starvation or suffocation in his black hole. Then there was a buzz, and a familiar brushing of his face. The buzz wavered, then faded. He followed its direction, stumbling and tripping, until he saw a light ahead.

Outside was astonishing. The spaciousness was overwhelming for a start, especially the sky, arching from horizon to horizon in terrifying immensity. Then there was the infinite variety. Millions of leaves and blades of grass, each one different, and more flowers than he could remember. But there was something missing. There was no movement, apart from the stirring of branches in the light wind, the quivering of leaves in currents of air, and the starts and slight sounds of adjustment to vegetal growth.

No insects scurried across leaves. No butterflies lolloped; no gnats danced in patches of shade. No greenfly grazed, and no clockwork ladybirds preyed on them. There were no birds flying, and no twittering and rustling in the hedgerows. He stood looking and listening, in the growing conviction that there was no animal life at all.

So it had happened. That there had been a cataclysm of some sort was obvious. He was not surprised. In his cell he had become quite accustomed to the idea that he might be the only person in the world, ministered to by the machine after everyone else had died in some natural or man-made catastrophe. He wondered which it had been. A war? Pestilence? An epidemic disease that fed on human contact? His bitter disappointment had a wry edge of satisfaction, but not because he still harboured resentment; he was simply relieved at not having to meet people.

But gradually, the realization that he would never see another human face began to weigh in his belly like a stone. Couldn't he be mistaken? He hurried towards the houses that he could see from the prison gates, but before he reached them he saw a crashed car with the remains of a corpse inside. He did not care to inspect the bundles that lay on street corners and in overgrown gardens, or to investigate the houses. Music was still playing in a supermarket. Evidently the electricity was still working here – there was, of course, no reason why the nuclear generators should not run till the dynamos burnt out. He tried a telephone and it granted him a dialling tone. He dialled all the numbers he could remember, but in every case got either no answer, or the 'unobtainable' signal.

He went back into the supermarket to collect a few provisions. In the deep-freeze section the corpse of a young woman leaned into a chest and grasped a packet of ice-cream. The upper part of her body was perfectly preserved, but neither the smooth tan of her nape, nor the hair that cascaded among the iced lollies and packets of raspberry ripple, shed any light on what had happened. There were several other corpses sprawled round the liquor shelves near the exit. He skirted them, collected a rucksack from the sports shop next door, and packed it with provisions and a sleeping bag. He also changed his prison jumpsuit for new clothes of slightly unfamiliar cut. A little further down the street, he loaded the rucksack into the boot of a decent-looking car that was standing on a garage forecourt, filled the tank with petrol, and started out of town.

The prison was in a remote province. He took the road back along the peninsula. He had not formulated what he intended to do, exactly, but it seemed only right to go home and see what had happened there. As the roads became wider, he drove faster, till he was roaring along the empty dual carriageway with the accelerator on the floor. Why not? There were no cars, apart from occasional wrecks – he glimpsed rags and bones as he passed – and thoughts of self-preservation seemed almost in bad taste. When he came to villages, he found last year's leaves drifted across the streets. Sometimes traffic lights were still working, and it was surprising how difficult it was to ignore them. Gradually he drove more slowly.

He stopped to fetch a bar of chocolate from a shop, and felt reluctant to continue. What was the point? He knew how it would be. He considered looking for a room in an hotel, but didn't fancy the idea of sleeping in a town, with withered corpses all round. He parked in a high street, and went looking for a paper shop where he might pick up – literally – a map. There was music playing again. He had become used to the fact that it hung round these dead habitations like a ghostly keening. This time it did not come from a shop, but from somewhere outside the town. Then it must be very loud. It sounded modern, but quite different from the bland drivel of the supermarkets.

He found his map, but before studying it he drove slowly in the direction of the thumping din. The sound led him to a roadhouse, where coloured lights still rotated slowly in the dusk. Projected images of war, city streets and frenetic dancers came and went on a group of screens set round an open-air platform. Tables were arranged under trees hung with fairy lights. It was bizarre, and he stopped to look. This was the nearest he had come to seeing living fellow humans since he had gone into solitary. He took a long pull at a bottle he had taken from an off-licence and tried to imagine that the image of a girl writhing in a spotlight was real.

The girl on the screen mimed the words of the song that was playing, slightly out of synchronization. Hands on hips, she rocked her pelvis, then pouted her lips, closed her eyes and drew up her shoulders as if in rapturous anticipation of a kiss. Her wide-topped blouse slid off one shoulder, and she arched her back, running her hands down her sides. Then, after a couple of convulsive and inept bump-and-grinds, she walked off the platform and flung herself into a chair at one of the tables in the half-dark circle.

He blinked, and looked again. The girl had – she had walked off! So she must really be alive!

His heart thumped painfully as he got out of the car and slowly approached under the loops of fairy-lights. 'He . . . Hello?' he called, and jumped at his own croaking.

The music faded, and this time he shouted more loudly, 'Hello?'

There was a gasp, and a chair clattered over as the girl leapt to her feet and stumbled between the tables.

'It's all right. I won't come any closer. I . . .' he realized he didn't know what to say.

'Who are you?' She sounded frightened; almost angry.

'Oh, sorry. Yes, of course. My name's Oates. People used to call me Titus but it's really George. George Oates. I've been in prison. May I sit down? I'll go away if you like.'

'No!'

Exhausted by the confrontation and by his longest conversation in years, George took that for dismissal, and turned back towards the car in obedient relief.

'I mean, don't go away! . . . Please!' And the girl rushed to grab hold of him. He drew away, but she crushed herself against him, sobbing and snorting into his new shirt.

He was horrified. It was too sudden and extreme a contact. He gritted his teeth as she boo-hooed wetly against his chest, then he forced himself, after one or two trial gestures, to pat her on the head. 'There, there,' he said. He was almost certain that was the right thing for such situations.

She looked up, snivelling, and wailed, 'I'm Sharon. I didn't think there was anyone else – I haven't seen anyone for . . .' and her face puckered up in a renewed imitation of a squashed fruit spurting juice.

He gave her a meal in a fast-food restaurant where there seemed no sign of any corpses. The microwaves worked, and the selection of ready dishes was quite good. The claret from the excellent wine merchant's opposite was even better. Sharon had stopped crying, and was extravagantly elated. George found that easier to cope with, but still difficult. He sneaked glances at her. With her red hair and soft, childish face, she was not what he thought of as his type. But she was his first human for – he asked her what year it was – seven years, so she was interesting.

Her eyes were on him with frank, almost avid, excitement. After a while, she reached out to touch his face. He turned, and watched her mouth as she spoke, wondering at the pink jewels of her gums, glimpsed between the paler pink chiselling of her lips. Her eyes were still slightly bloodshot from crying. That was to be expected, but he was startled by their blueness. He had quite forgotten that animals could have blue bits.

He told his story quickly – it was simple enough. When he explained how he had become accustomed to being alone, she burst in with, 'But not to the idea that there was no one else left in the world!'

'Oh, yes,' he said. 'It seemed just like that, most of the time,' and she reached out and squeezed his hand.

Her story was more complicated. She told it from her bed in the hotel room they chastely shared because she could not bear to be alone again.

She had been on a trip to the famous caves not far from here. Did he know them? Well, it didn't matter. They were very deep, with an underground lake and those things: stalactites and stalagmites. It wasn't very exciting, but it was the most popular outing in the area, and all the incomers went there at least once. The incomers were people who came out here because of the tension, and then because of the 'Nearly War'. In those days TV and radio were jammed to such an extent that people had to make their own entertainment or go back to simple pleasures, like trips to caves. Anyway, while they were in the caves there had been tremors, and the water in the lake had come in a great wave, and – well, she'd been scared and had run the wrong way, you see, so she got separated.

The lights had gone out, and there was water one way and fallen rocks the other. After stumbling about and screaming for help for hours, she had blundered upon the chairs and tables of the underground snack bar, and she had lived there on hamburgers and fizzy drinks, for she didn't know how long. After what must have been days she found a light switch that worked – perhaps it was the emergency system. But then she daren't turn it off, so she didn't know if it was night or day. Could he imagine?

He nodded into the lovely darkness. 'Yes,' he said.

She was there for ages. The hamburgers ran out – she was sick of them, anyway – and so did the hot dogs. There were some bits of mouldy cheese and some doughnuts, all withered with age. She was drinking the lake water by then. All the time there were tremors, and sometimes more rockfalls. She used to sit and listen to the cave falling down all round her. Then, when she was asleep, there was an enormous crash, with rocks coming down everywhere, and suddenly a draught of cold air. She followed that, till she saw a light, and found people.

At first she thought they had come to rescue her, then she saw they were in a bad way themselves, all blotchy, and wobbly on their legs, and they said they were fugitives. They told her how the wireless had finally faded out. It had been coming and going for days, with reports of rocket attacks, orders that everyone must stay where they were, and a lot of stuff about contamination. The fugitives had talked about thick banks of cloud, and the rain. There seemed to have been a lot of rain, all in different colours. No, it was true! There was one rain that went on for days and they called it the 'blue rinse'. It was wonderful how they made jokes, sick as they were. There was a rain of blood – or so they called it – and one of dead insects. Then the birds began to drop out of the sky. They said it got really horrible after that.

She had lived with them, near the mouth of the caves, for a long time. They almost worshipped her, because she wasn't dying. The young men were dangerous at first, but the women looked after her. Soon they all seemed to be old, anyway. They died one by one. A man who had been a professor told her it was probably safe to go outside. He died, too, of course. She stayed at the cave as long as there was anyone to look after. Then food was getting short, and she couldn't stay with the corpses. Not after the last of the children. Coming here had been easy. There were abandoned cars everywhere. But she had been going mad before he came. He'd seen her at it, hadn't he? Imagine! She'd been running that disco system night after night and falling asleep with it going full blast.

'I think you did wonderfully,' said George, thinking of the horror of the cave.

'Yeah. I like dancing', she said.

George was surprised at how well they got on. He would have expected to have been irritated by her refusing to let him out of her sight, but in fact he found the sight of her equally reassuring. She really had quite a trim little figure, seen now from behind, as she scrambled in and out of the cars in a showroom.

'I like this one,' she said, emerging from a Rolls. Her face was quite amiable, too, a bit like a Renoir.

'It's yours,' he said. 'Take us to the seaside.'

He was still discovering the excitement of having a companion. He had already discovered the wonderful convenience and aptness of her body. He had thought a lot about that sort of thing in prison; at least, at first. Now he realized he had known nothing about it – which was perhaps why the topic had palled long before he got out. Nowadays, he thought about it quite a lot again. And she was there, and willing!

Wrapped up with each other as they were, it began to seem an idyllic life. Sharon still found the quietness uncanny, but after the white noise George loved the real silence with all its sounds: twigs cracking; buds snapping open; leaves moving against each other. He longed for some animal noise, though. Sometimes he thought he heard other men speaking. Then his heart leapt with excitement – and fear of rivals.

For the most part they went about quietly, avoiding towns and places that were redolent of vanished life. At first they did go in for sudden outbursts of noise: racing cars on the motorway, bathing in the sea with uninhibited whoops and screams, playing music – his Beethoven and her Pop – full blast. But those things were becoming less attractive. They had settled in a house overlooking the sea. There, they cultivated the garden, against the moment when the cans in the supermarket would all start to leak. He read books and secretly worried about how the plants were managing without bees. Sharon sewed, as if there weren't clothes enough in the shops. They were almost content in their Eden.

*

THE FLY

'Listen!'

They were eating dessert when Sharon froze with her spoon half-way to her raspberry-stained mouth and commanded again, 'Listen, George!'

George listened, and thought he could hear a faint sound, but it faded. Sharon held up her finger for silence. The sound came and went again. Then there was a familiar buzz in his ear, and he glimpsed a swerving atom dancing away. Finally, with a sudden blip of noise, followed by silence, a black spot settled on his bowl.

'It's my fly!' he shouted.

Sharon was amazed, then immediately sceptical. 'How do you know it's the same one?'

'It's the only one, isn't it? I mean . . . I recognize it!' and he pointed to the glinting green-black body, the bulbous eyes, the hairiness when you looked close – only he daren't look too close for fear of frightening it – and yes! 'It's got a chipped wing. Look! It is my fly,' he crowed.

'Fancy it finding us!' said Sharon.

There may have been a touch of resentment in her voice, almost as if she were jealous of the fly. But then she became as excited as he was at this meeting with another living creature, and she soaked sugar in raspberry juice for its feast of welcome.

George continued to be surprised at his own contentment. If he sometimes felt the lack of companionship with a trained mind, he was just as often delighted by Sharon's trick of being unanswerably right for the wrong reasons. If he thought wistfully of other faces, she would astonish him with her changeability; her mouth could remind him, now of a Renoir, now of the girl on the magazines that were fading in the news-stands, now of a film actress he had adored long ago. In any case, after so long alone, he could never have coped with more than one person at a time. What was more, given a choice, Sharon might not have chosen him. As it was, he was pleasantly aware that she worshipped the ground he trod.

Sharon had wanted to keep the fly safe somewhere, but George would not have it confined a second time. It seemed grateful, for it stayed with them, scribbling its dance under a nearby branch, or sitting, contemplating their images among the hundred others collected by its compound eyes. Presumably it was happy too.

'I knew it!' Sharon shouted.
  'Knew what, darling?'
  'There *are* two of them. Look!'
George looked, saw one fly, then saw it somewhere else, then saw two together.
  'Good Lord!' he said. 'It's found a mate.'
  'Like us,' cooed Sharon.
George liked the idea of his old companion having its own good fortune.
  'Lucky he wasn't a spider,' he said, 'or she might have eaten him. I wonder where she came from,' and he smiled benignly on the two flies dancing together under the overhang of the balcony.

But a few days later it became clear that there were not just two flies, but three or four . . . or even five. Then it became a dozen, and then it was, well, it was a bloody plague, said Sharon, as she threw out a maggoty joint of meat. George swore, and smote the busy air. Sharon asked what he was going to do about it and, while he was deciding, fetched flyspray from the supermarket.

Thereafter they lived in a sickening aura of insecticide, but there was still a haze of buzzing atoms about their heads wherever they went. Black entities leapt away from every surface they approached. Flies blundered into their mouths. Flies pursued them, eager to drink their sweat. There was a constant monotone hum, blended from thousands of notes manifesting different speeds, directions and degrees of excitement. George explained that, of course, there was plenty

THE FLY

of ripe fruit about, but since the animal corpses had all rotted or dried up long ago, and since the two of them were the only warm-blooded creatures alive . . .

And of course, there were no predators.

George nailed netting over the windows. It was a beautiful Indian summer, but they could not go outside. Indoors, they were beseiged, with flies beating on the glass Sharon had morning sickness, and the flyspray made it worse. She cried a lot. George stuffed the chimneys and cracks, but every time a door was opened a cloud of flies rushed in. Walking was impossible. At first, fast driving brought relief, because the flies were left behind. But as the swarms became thicker, the car scooped them up until the air intakes were blocked.

They went out in a boat and lay blissfully unpestered, about a mile offshore, for half a day until the flies found them. George said that suggested a way out. They must go abroad. They would set off at night, in a small boat, to minimize the risk of taking flies with them. Across the Channel they could transfer to something bigger, and head for the Mediterranean. 'Think of it!' said George. 'It'll be like the morning of the world.' He made it sound ideal, with a better climate and easier living. It would be like it had been at first – only better still.

The engine stopped shortly after daybreak. They were out of sight of land, and there was no sign of flies. All the same, George said the trouble was probably dead flies in the carburettor. The boat wasn't all that small, and the engine was heavy. He wasn't going to risk losing it into the sea, so he worked on the carburettor with the engine in place. It was flies, all right: the filter was bunged-up. He told Sharon it would only take a few minutes and, leaning over the stern, he carefully unscrewed one of the jets. Best make a proper job of it!

'Oh, no!' Sharon's scream made him jump, and her recoil across the boat caused quite a lurch. The combined effect of both was that the slightly oily jet slipped through his fingers, and the soft suckings of the sea under the boat were punctuated by a 'plop'.

Sharon was squirting insecticide. 'One just landed on me. I think I got it, but you'd better hurry up!'

'Keep calm and try not to rock the boat about, then!' George didn't mention the lost jet, but began to search the toolbox for a spare. There must be one somewhere.

'There's another!' Sharon was busy with the spray again, and weeping. Soon the stink of the stuff lay heavily on the boat, and the surrounding water was covered with an oily scum of dead flies. George told Sharon about the jet, and that there wasn't a spare.

'What shall we do?'

'There's a pair of oars.'

He rowed into the heat of the day, going as hard as he could. When he had to rest Sharon took over. Lying exhausted in the stern, looking up through the dancing black specks, George thought they might be getting fewer. But by nightfall it was clear that they were not. More and more flies were arriving. By now they were crawling about on the bodies of the dead ones that carpeted the sea. He told Sharon there was no point in choking themselves with more spraying. The flies that had already arrived would stay all night, and tomorrow more would come. Not daring to undress, they crept into their sleeping bags with their clothes on. Then they were unbearably hot, so they crawled out again and covered themselves in light blankets. Sharon was sobbing quietly.

George woke from a sleep of sheer weariness. It was barely light and he lay for a while, looking at the still form of Sharon across the boat. He suddenly raised his head in alarm. Since the coming of the flies they had both evolved a habit of constant motion, even in sleep – of twitchings, tossings, and flickings of hands against faces, until their 'St Flytus's dance' had become a wry joke like the 'blue rinse' rain of the fugitives in Sharon's cave. But Sharon was lying quite motionless.

THE FLY

She had let her blanket slip and lay uncovered like a statue. But it was a statue of coal: rough-skinned and glintingly granular. George groaned as he realized that she was encased from head to toe in flies. He raised himself on one elbow, and saw that black extensions ran from her arms into the bottom of the boat: flies were investing the blood that had flowed from the wrists she had slashed with her scissors. George backed to the side of the boat, which tipped towards him. Sharon's body pitched forward and the flies rose in a cloud. George recoiled further and fell backwards into the sea.

It may even have been deliberate. At any rate, he was glad to find himself there. He swam rapidly away from the boat, at first to escape the crusty scum of dead flies that surrounded it, then simply to escape. He ducked his head under water frequently as he swam, and looked back over his shoulder occasionally, till the boat was out of sight. Then he swam slowly on, still brushing his face occasionally. He was becoming tired and the water was cold. It was definitely very cold. Summer was over; he had noticed that the trees had begun to turn some time ago. He knew this was an inane conversation to be having with himself, still, it passed the time...

'Soon it will be winter.' He thought the words to the rhythm of his swimming. He tried to think about winter in an effort not to think about flies. And then it came to him: 'Where do flies go in the winter time?' Soon it would be winter – then soon there would be no flies!

'Sharon!' His reproachful cry was cut short by choking as two flies entered his mouth.

He turned back for the boat. Another month would do it. If he could only get back to shore and stick it out for only four more weeks. He tried to raise himself in the water to see in which direction the boat lay, but he saw only pale waves and the horizon. He swam on, more slowly. Twice his face sank into the water, and twice he raised it, spluttering, and made a few more fitful strokes. His face dropped into the water again and his back rose to compensate. The island of his shoulders bobbed in the gentle swell. A fly landed on it and was soon joined by another. More came, hovering and settling, until there was only a mass of metallic green-black flotsam, glinting and slowly stirring in the rays of the rising sun. A low murmuring sound rose from hundreds of quivering wings, each with a small chip missing.

SAINTS' HOLIDAY
John Kerr

After six weeks we were down to three: me, Harry and Bob. The rest had gone home to Mammy. But we weren't for any of that. Gazing at the letterbox waiting for the giro; sipping half pints of lager making them last all night; watching the pox on the box with maw, paw, and the weans. No way.

We were in Europe. We were the youth of Europe camped on a jasmine-scented Greek isle, the jack boot of tourism, right up the cradle of civilization. One hitch, not a drach among us.

Pelekas wasn't for Mr Average Tourist. The ramshackle old village teetered on the edge of a steep cliff. It only took twenty minutes to scrabble down the dirt track to the beach, but it was a two hour, slow climb back. And the only place to escape the suffocating heat was that sea.

But the nude bathing and the parties that Spiros hosted at his caff had started a buzz. Hitchhikers would whisper Pelekas to each other and smile dreamily. Yank students would find the word scrawled on the covers of their Bible, *Cheat Your Way Round Europe*. Aussies would trade the name for a VW head gasket. Pelekas drew a good crowd.

The locals called us the pink bottoms. They hated us and who could blame them.

That day we were on the beach trying to hustle some cash. Spiros would give us fruit that a big hotel had chucked out and we would split the cash we made on it. You know the kind of stuff people sell on the beach: mushy peaches, rancid watermelon slices, grapes with wasps in them. We even filled old plastic bottles from the local well and claimed it was pure Swiss spring. If you held it to the light I swear you could see the bugs.

But we sold more than you'd think. I've a good sales technique for nude beaches. Harry was a six footer and ugly with it. With his peeling nose, footballing tattoos and blotches of sunburn he wasn't a pretty sight in a loincloth. Harry would stand and look. Now everyone's ashamed of their body. Nobody thinks they're the 'right shape'. And Harry served to remind them of their imperfections. The girls would get twitchy over their boobs or their tummies and reach for their purse. And the men? Just a wry smile and a confidential whisper then man and boy they rolled on to their stomachs and paid their drachs.

Only one guy never paid, Matt, a wee black bloke. He was AWOL from one of Uncle Sam's subs in Spain so he said. The first day he appeared we tried the long stare and a low whistle. Nothing. Harry spoke. 'That suntan oil has fairly done you some good Jim.'

A deep grin split Matt's face. As he stood up I saw the grains of white sand sparkle on his coal-black skin. He examined the fruit carefully and shook his head. Then, very casually, he lifted Harry, tattoos and all, turned him upside down and shook out the coins. Next he tore off Harry's loincloth and set fire to it claiming it was a public health risk. All this stark bollock naked. We left him alone after that.

I watched him every day as he basked in the sun, nostrils flaring in the heat. Matt claimed he'd paid for that tan. At night he wasn't a bad lad, told some jokes and danced a lot.

'If you weren't poor we could be friends, Mugzay,' he'd say. I was touched.

On the beach we had hit a problem. Bob dropped the tray. Now sandy, rancid watermelon was something even I couldn't shift so we started the long trek back to the taverna. In the dust and heat we weren't the best of companions.

'We ain't got no money,' intimated Harry and Bob with monotonous regularity.

'*Per ardua ad astra*,' I replied. But I had to think of something.

Bob was running about swiping with his hand at something and this waste of precious energy was getting on my nerves.

'There's a bug after me,' he told us.

'Let it land,' said Harry.

Bob stood still and a dirty black monster swooped in on his back.

'Go on. Get it.' But Harry waited till it bit Bob before squeezing it between thumb and forefinger. A black squidgy mess.

'It bit me.'

'Aye, but it won't bite anyone else.'

Harry could be a real bastard.

Near the village a fleet of rented mopeds buzzed us, kicking up more dust. Only people with money could rent bikes. Germans to a man I thought. Madge was with them, too.

'Come on Mugzay. Put your back into it,' she yelled in her nasal drawl. I had fucked her the previous week. She was a mixed-up Australian about thirty (but what side of thirty I asked myself), a student who kept going vague on what her subject was. She was a good-looking woman, big with dark eyes that swallowed you up and bright pearly gnashers. She talked all the time. But the noise she made in bed.

Well, for a start we were on the ground in a tent surrounded by twenty other tents. And she's going huh, huh, HUH, aiee. Well, okay, I don't mind. But pretty soon half the bloody camp is going huh, huh, HUH, aiee. And she gets louder and they get louder. And there's now fifty people going huh, huh, HUH, aiee as loud as they can get. And I just can't go on. I get out the tent and shout bloody hell at the whole lot. They all laugh and Madge laughs loudest.

All that week Matt tried to change my name to 'Steamtrain'. But I like Mugzay cause it doesn't mean anything.

So we slouched along to the village and found the Greeks

were actually doing something. Usually the old men sat about in the bar playing chequers and spitting, and the women squatted on the stone steps, clutching their rosaries. But in the main square they were working away like devils building something out of wood. For an odd moment I thought they were making a gallows. You get scared sometimes when you're not in your own country, like everyone's gone mad save you. You never know what's going on. Never can tell. They ignored us as we gawped but that was nothing new. And still Harry and Bob were grumbling. I had to think of something spectacular.

Spiros told us what the good townsfolk were up to when we got to the taverna. The *feste*. Every September the yokels dig up their patron saint, St Spiridion, wrap a few blankets round the bits they've got left, stick him in a silver box and charge up and down the main street to scare off the devils. Then they have a dance and get ratarsed. My gallows was a dance platform.

Spiros ran his taverna solely for the pink bottoms. It was a good place, dirty but cheap. From the beer garden you could plunge 200 feet straight into the Adriatic. That bright, dazzling blue stuff was almost too tempting, and after I'd been swilling the yellow beer I made sure I kept a good distance from the edge.

He had been to catering college in Athens and was a man of ideas. Tarts and priests, discos, donkey trekking, three-legged scuba diving. He had the ideas but he did nothing except screw the young tourists, promising them undying love and a job in the kitchen. Both of these were lies as his mum did all the cooking.

'If you'd been Greek, Mugzay, you too would be big figure in tourism industry.' But I was born in Falkirk and we were a bit short on the industries front.

He told me about his first lesson in the English language learned at a tender age and never forgotten:

> I fuck the fat one,
> You fuck the fat one,

SAINTS' HOLIDAY

> He fucks the fat one,
> We fuck the fat one,
> You fuck the fat one.
> The fat one fucks.
> I've got his number.

Anyway, Spiros wanted his share of the fruit selling. He didn't like the story of Bob falling on the sand any more than I did. Harry tried the 'We've bought you some empty bottles trick.' There are only so many times you can steal a crate of empty bottles from around the back and hawk them to the owner. The first time is all right. Then they get suspicious. Then they get mad. Spiros was foaming. We were going to end our holiday at the foot of the cliff if Simon hadn't intervened.

I promise Simon is the last guy I'll mention. He was in his late thirties, thick black beard, pale watery skin, an aesthete whatever that means. He rolled his own did Simon.

He listened a lot, never said much but used his round almond eyes to probe deep into your soul. In the dead time of night I told him things I'd said to no one. About how I could take our old damp house and its fousty furniture and crush it in my fist, burn out the waste and decay and tear down the whole fucking town. And he would sit and nod, dead serious, and take in all that anger. What he did with it God alone knows.

When he wasn't listening he was sweeping. Simon swept the bar for Spiros. Never touched the food, just swept the tables, talked to the lizards and gazed out to sea. Spiros was always teasing him. He would hide his brush, tell him how many hearts he'd broken that day, jump on his back. Once he even bought a vacuum from town and insisted on a race. But Simon didn't join in. Kept working at his job and smiled kindly at Spiros as he danced with his hoover.

Simon was good for another thing. He was always good for three beers. He sat with us and explained patiently about the *feste*, the primitive magic, how the land was gouged from the sea and how the sea would reclaim the souls. Lots of stuff like that. We listened politely. If a man buys you a beer you have to listen to him. Then he went quiet and went back to his sweeping.

Cold beer was what I needed to sort out our predicament. Huddled together I told Harry and Bob the plan.

'It's the *feste*.'

They nodded.

'The Greeks get drunk and drink brings out their national characteristic.' They nodded like their heads were coming off.

'What are the Greeks famous for?' I asked.

'Philosophers?'

'Kebabs?' volunteered Bob.

They weren't going to get it. Five thousand years of civilization had passed them by.

'The Greeks are famed for their thieving.'

'So?'

'So we lift old Madge's money belt in the middle of all the fun.'

'They'll know it was us.'

'Normally they would suspect us. But we say it was the drunken thieving Greeks.'

They thought.

'She must have fifty quid in that belt. She'll be pissed. It'll be a dawdle.' I could see the cogs and levers of their minds going round in stately fashion.

'Well?'

'Okay,' said Harry.

'Bob?'

'We shouldn't steal from her.'

'You can go home if you want to.'

'It doesn't feel right.' But I knew he was in. He was just cross we had let that bug bite him.

That night a mass of us went down the square to watch the old wrinklies let their hair down. As could be guessed, they couldn't organize a piss up in a brewery. The square was packed with Greeks, there were firecrackers, a folk band and dancing, but this was a one-road town. The traffic still had to go through the square. Buses and lorries jammed in honking and revving right on top of the dancers.

Then there was the food. Some worthy had elected our Spiros to provide the old victuals. Naturally they hadn't arrived.

To finish it off old St Spiridion fell out of his coffin on the last lap to the church. This according to Simon was a very bad omen and there was a great lamentation and gnashing of teeth from the congregation. But it suited us in our skulduggery. Harry's IQ was about room temperature and we're talking centigrade, but with half a razor blade he could be as skilful as any surgeon. A surge forward by the crowd as the dance picks up. A glint of light on steel and a deft incision on Madge's money belt. Then two podgy fingers slip inside. For an awful moment I think he's cut too deep and he's in her stomach, but as he withdraws those fingers there's a nice quality wallet between them and Madge is smiling as much as Harry.

That wallet had one thousand dollars in it. One thousand dollars. What the hell was she doing in a place like that with one thousand dollars? She could have had a bed in a hotel, eaten proper food, had a shower. She could have had air conditioning.

We could retire on a thousand dollars.

We rejoined the gang back at the taverna. Thirteen of us strung out in a line behind a bare wooden table. Spiros felt so guilty about lousing up the food that he broke out some vinegar red and hard pitta bread. Simon poured for us all and broke some bread and the sun fell into the sea like a fiery ball.

But it was a solemn party. Something was troubling our merry throng. A deep foreboding. One prat even brought out a guitar and they would have started on 'Blowing in the Wind' and snivelling about '68. Then something extraordinary happened. Three Greek gods strode into the bar.

Blank white plaster masks, empty eye sockets, naked bodies painted gold and silver. Each carried a flaming torch in one hand and a spear in the other.

Nobody moved. In the half light they were statues, avenging furies. Down below us in the village an odd cackle of laughter floated up. Swinging back and forward they pointed with their spears at each one of us, accusing us silently. We sat frozen. At last someone did something. Matt pulled himself up to his full five foot four and strode over.

'The three wise men right?' But his voice was cracked and I could see the perspiration on his brow.

'Do you think they've come about the purse?' whispered Bob.

I ground my heel into the soft arch of his foot. With a loud shriek the spears jerked out and up ending barely an inch from Matt's throat.

The three gods advanced chanting a weird whooping noise. Matt was being prodded before the spears, back towards the edge and that long drop. Nobody moved. But as they came into the light I saw it was Spiros beneath the mask. And I broke the spell. He must have slipped away when the guitar was brought out.

We all laughed about it, but it wasn't meant to be funny and everyone knew it. Spiros mumbled shit and threw his hands up. A joke's a joke. How can you explain them? Funny folk those Greeks. Simon tried to calm things down but the party broke up soon after.

At dawn Madge kicked our tent down and using some pretty damn fine language started tearing her way through our things. Obviously she was missing the purse. But it didn't do any good of course, we had buried it the previous night.

The rest of the camp stood in a half circle with accusation written all over their faces. We looked as plaintive as possible as Madge ransacked our paltry transactions.

'I had eighty dollars in that wallet,' she screamed.

Lying bitch.

SAINTS' HOLIDAY

We put forward our case. We didn't have any money. We hadn't spent any money. We were going home. How come we were to blame?

What about the Krauts? That was a good move. They were big, stupid and bad-tempered. They rose magnificently to the bait. Come on. Who invaded Poland? Tell me that. Who started the war? They were getting mad.

All it needed was a slow chant of 'Uber Alles' and a sausage eater lunged with a left hook. In the mêlée that followed the three of us held our own against tough odds. Simon and Matt eventually broke it up. Torn and bleeding we looked even more innocent.

Madge turned her fury on the camp in general. How could we betray her? After all she'd done for us. It was a magnificent tirade against an unjust world.

One thousand dollars and she hadn't bought a drink all month. I would have loved to have spiked her speech but they would have crucified me on the spot.

Bob dropped the 'thieving Greeks' solution into the conversation. As usual the 'Boy Wonder' got the timing totally wrong. I had to respond that Madge had probably spent the money on some Greek boy to do the business. More tears from Madge and cries of bad form from the crowd.

After that snippet of taste and decency we shuffled off to the beach, hurt and huffed that we should be so maligned, leaving Matt and Simon to cope with the amateur dramatics. So we sat on the beach for a few hours not saying much, feeling low. It was Harry who saw the smoke first in the fields beyond the village. Then the flames reared up. Forty-foot red dragons galloped through the scrub, roaring out their anger.

The Greeks panicked. Preparing for the *feste* had nothing on this. Sea planes gouged out sea water and bombed the fires from the sky. Toddlers beat out flames with sticks. Old women, blackened by smoke, used blankets. They fought like crazies. Fire was the thing villagers feared the most. A single fire could wipe out a thousand year village in half a day, lay waste the olive groves and vines for decades, bring a curse of a hundred years.

So it was no surprise to learn that fire raising was a serious crime. And they didn't use the local traffic cop. A young detective from Athens, with a sad droopy moustache, herded all the pink bottoms into the bar. He lectured about forty of us on morals and the fragile nature of Greek peasant life. Interesting stuff. And very quietly he tiptoed round the subject of fire raising and ever so softly asked who did it.

Now we all knew this was the business. This wasn't: 'We're going to kick you round the cell and get the embassy to pack you off in a plane.' They were going to lock someone away.

Someone, and they were sure it was a pink bottom, had brought bad luck into the village. They wanted that person. Hands up who wants whipped. And Simon stood forward. Right next to me he took one pace forward. How could he do it? No way would Simon ever start a fire. Why did he want to take the blame? Christ...

Luckily the detective wasn't a stupid man. He hardly gave Simon a second glance as his gaze settled on a very shaky Madge. He went over and led her gently out. She started to sob. Her shoulders hunched up in her neck. I looked at Simon then Madge and felt...

But God knows why she did it. If she had a thousand dollars she must have been able to get more. Why sling a can of petrol about? What good could that do? She was muttering on about the fates. What was that?

And Simon. Why did he stand forward? I'm not educated. I did ten sodding years in a comprehensive. But I'm sharp. I've learned from life's cruel blows. What did they know? He didn't even like her. What was this big step for mankind for?

A few weeks later we were on another island – Poxos or Herpes – or something like that and we still had a bit of dough. I stood on a beach and a young girl buckled up my harness. Then she made a little salute and a surf boat roared forward. It jerked me and the parachute straight up in the sky. With both my arms pulled right back and the sun beating down on my face I felt alive. I was going to soar higher and higher and touch my god, pull his white beard right off.

And for a second I knew what Simon felt. I felt it.

But you only get five minutes. Then you fall in the sea.

'One of the old school', 'a grand old lady', 'a formidable character' . . . such were the euphemisms customarily applied to mark out, like warning signs, the territory of her crusty and dogmatic personality. She had taught at a missionary school in India for thirty years and her husband had died there. I knew only the crotchety remainder of her life that poked awkwardly into the present like the tip of an iceberg, a hazard to modern shipping (as the Reverend McKenzie could testify). Sometimes, though, I had a sense of a whole life of which I knew nothing, a hidden presence looming large below the surface.

As her only nephew (and therefore, in her eyes, automatically preferable to a whole brace of nieces), Aunt Mary made me her sole executor and left me the residue of her estate, the bulk of which (a tiny amount) went back to the mission in Bangalore where she had spent her working life. The 'residue' was well-named, for without the tide of Aunt Mary's animating presence, all the objects in the flat she rented seemed to have been left high and dry, like faint watermarks, a powdery whiteness of brine staining the wall of a deserted harbour.

Most of her things I gave away to cousins. Not that there was much; Aunt Mary had lived a frugal life and there was little except a wardrobe of clothes, some china ornaments, a shelf of dusty theological books and various oddments from her life in India – a couple of faded photographs, a box of evangelical tracts in what looked like Punjabi and a battered writing case. I was surprised to find how much I missed her as I organized the disposal of this frail accumulation of flotsam. Like some long accustomed marker buoy, Aunt Mary had floated in her swell of years, blinking occasional reminders of age to a younger generation. Now I felt that I had lost an important landmark from which, almost without noticing, I had taken many bearings.

Chief among the mementos which I kept was a beautiful bronze statuette. The near-naked male figure it portrayed was about fifteen inches tall, slim, elegant and draped in the finest of robes. However the thing had been cast or sculpted,

THE LOTUS-BLOSSOM JESUS

the artist had somehow managed to give the robe a delicately flowing effect so that the figure seemed to be striding smoothly forward. One arm was extended with the hand held palm upwards, the other fell relaxed by the figure's side. The face was faintly smiling, with delicately chiselled oriental features. The whole impression given was one of immense serenity and poise.

Aunt Mary had nothing but contempt for most eastern art (indeed for most art full stop). It was either out and out idolatry or a frivolous distraction from the important things in life (work and prayer). But she had always treasured this particular piece. It was, she explained to me more than once, an Indian Christ, bearing the stigmata on his palm and striding towards the doubting Thomases of this world to chasten their unbelief. She had been given it during her husband's fatal illness (he died of typhoid in 1926). Aunt Mary had kept vigil by his bedside and one terrible night had wavered on the brink of unbelief as she watched his life ebb away. How could God allow such useless suffering? But even as she drifted into a fog of hopelessness and began to doubt the very foundations of her faith, her eyes fell on the statuette of the Indian Christ, standing calm, compassionate and commanding on the bedside table. It had, so she believed, saved her from the sin of despair.

In her retirement, the bronze had always occupied pride of place in her flat. Incongruous in its utter foreignness, it stood like some strange figurehead on the mantelpiece in her living room, suggesting voyages to far-off places. I sometimes pictured Aunt Mary as a young woman, sitting by her husband's bedside in the tropical heat, her brow damp with sweat, her eyes, red-rimmed from weeping, looking every now and then to the cool, serene figure of her Indian Christ. Somehow, into the depths of her sadness, an unknown artist had thrown a life belt for her faith, just at that moment when it seemed bound to sink and leave her utterly bereft.

*

SURVIVORS
Susan Chaney

When Liam was born it was winter. I remember the hollow sound of the dead leaves blowing outside my window. I may have forgotten a great deal else, but I will always remember the sound of the leaves.

Time has passed since then. Sometimes I think the hardest part of being here is simply enduring the passing of time. Time must be shifted so painstakingly, so thoroughly, like radioactive contamination. We have a clock on the wall but it stopped some time ago. We are not concerned with clocks. We have nowhere to go, no appointment to keep. Somehow we know intuitively when it is time for food, for drink, for medication, exercise or rest.

There have been fine days, a few hours of weak sun when I lay all day and watched the frosty red shadows creep across the wall. There has been snow. I have heard the gardeners outside stamping it from their boots, each sound intensified by the quiet.

It is still cold, the nurses still complain about the weather but I think that we are edging towards spring. I think it must be February. The light lingers a while longer around the windows. In the nurses' office is a blue ceramic bowl with the spiky tips of hyacinths just showing. I have touched them with my fingers. My fingertips send messages to my brain which tell me that new growth comes with the spring, but my skin absorbs the light. My skin finds it creamy, it holds a promise. I lean helpless towards the light. I think light with my skin.

The fact of the hyacinths, the sensation of the light. The correlation of the two tells me that I am still intact. I am still surviving.

garments. Skeins of wool in bold primary colours tumbled off my lap. I wanted my baby to be bright, to be strong. I thought of names like Zoë and Zelda. I was so smug, so sure. I would say to my friends, 'Yes, she's a girl. Yes, I love her already. Yes, I knew the minute she was conceived,' and they would laugh and say, 'Silly thing, that's impossible,' but they would drop their eyes in the face of my conviction.

This place is full of women. 'Why is this place full of women?' I asked the doctor. 'Why do you make them sleep so much? Why do you give them plastic knives and forks? Why do they eat blancmange and baked beans like children?'

'Well, Mrs Ashcroft,' he replied over his glasses. 'Women are more susceptible to mental illness. One in six women will spend some time in a mental institution.'

'Illness, illness,' I repeated. 'There is no illness, no sickness or health, there's only the failure of love. These women are here to escape from love. Love is made safe here, is reduced to visiting hours, fresh flowers on the bedside table, pretty nighties and fluffy dressing gowns. Love is made concern. Love is made manageable.'

When I came the women gathered round me, rapping their hollow fingers against me like twigs on a window pane, but I was not afraid of them. I have always known them.

'You won't be here long dearie, will you? Things at home just got on top of you didn't they? Not like us. Many of us might never leave.'

I am not afraid of them because I have always known them. I am transparent and I dissolve effortlessly into them. That's why I like it here. We exist independent of our past, released from our history.

There's old Mrs Pickering with her crimplene dress, her lumpy purple legs, her mangled slippers. She carries on an ancient quarrel with her brother, Ralph, dead these twenty years. I hear her querulous old voice, accusing, berating, scolding, pleading, complaining. At night, when she eventually quietens, she falls asleep sobbing for her mother.

I think of my own children, Zoë asleep in bed at home,

tiny Liam in the hospital nursery. The one I loved so much that when she was born music rocked her cradle. The other I could not love at all. Suppose they wake in the night and cry for me, I will not come.

Then there's Gina, pretty little Gina with her black silk shawl, containing many colours like a bird's wing. She's given up talking and would give up eating too if they would let her. She sits by the window, her knees drawn up to her chin, rocking, rocking herself continuously. I have come behind her and bent myself over her back, my face against her neck, my arms along her own, and I have rocked with her and listened to her voices, they stirred inside her like bells in the water. Her voices eat into me, they are acid with her grief.

'Michael says I am his star child. He filled my room with flowers just to see the blossoms hang like lanterns in my eyes. Michael says I am his time-traveller. Michael says let's take a trip, let's have an interstellar rainy day. Michael says, "For Christ's sake woman, pull yourself together. Look at the mess in here. Look at the state of the children. You've forgotten to do the shopping again. What do you do all day?" Michael says, "I can't cope with you, I've had enough." I don't recognize Michael any more.'

The nurses are all fond of Gina. She causes them so little trouble. We are all fond of Gina. We take turns to feed her and brush her long dark hair. We play with her like a doll. Tessa calls her 'our little acid head'.

Today I am wearing Sadie's dress. Sadie must be sixty-five but she believes she's still a girl. She's shy, confiding, coy, cajoling. She likes to show me mementoes of her past, her treasures and artifacts spread across her bed for my inspection.

Sadie favours bright colours. This morning she was wearing a scarlet mini skirt, her tights fell in wrinkles around her skinny ankles. She had silver lurex socks printed with bright blue stars. Her tiny fingers were weighted with rings. 'Look dear,' she said, rummaging in the back of her cupboard. 'This dress will suit you. See how cunningly it's

'Mrs Ashcroft,' she said firmly. 'You'll just have to learn to love your baby. Have you never experienced the growth of love?' I think of my husband, my daughters, lovers I have known. I shout inside, 'No, no, I haven't. Love came immediately. Love was a wild flowering for me.'

I heard her voice float down. 'He's such a lovely baby. Did you know he had auburn hair?' This arrested me. I've always wanted a baby with russet hair, russet hair and freckled skin. I stop to think.

Why should she even notice the colour of his hair? Why should she call him lovely? 'Do you have children?' I demanded.

She passed her hand across her face. 'No. I haven't had time for a family. It's still very tough for a woman in this profession. You see,' she continued sadly, 'there's always a price. Now good day, Mrs Ashcroft. I'm a busy woman and you have some thinking to do.' She glanced dismissively at her watch and I left.

Tessa has gone, her bed is empty. It looks huge and forbidding, the white spread stretched firmly across it undisturbed by the smallest wrinkle. It reminds me of the icing on a wedding cake. I half expect to see a sugar bride and groom go waltzing across it, heading towards eternal bliss. She has discharged herself. She's left nothing for me, no note or indication of where she's gone.

Towards morning I woke. It was so quiet it startled me. The highly polished floor unrolled like an eerie green bandage beneath the exhausted night lights. The grim metal trolleys lined along the wall looked faintly luminous.

I reached down and touched my stomach. I was puzzled. It felt so hollow, it felt so wrong. I sucked in my breath hard until it felt as if my backbone were pressing into the sheet. It felt all wrong inside as if things were unfinished, the nerve endings snipped and tied with cat gut, the veins sealed. I had a baby. There should be a baby swelling and hardening beneath my hands. Something strong and bright had taken root. At last I knew what to do. I would put him back where he belonged. I sat up in bed and pushed the bell as hard as I could. The nurse came running.

'I want my baby, bring my baby here. Please bring my baby now.' She hurried away. She had been waiting for this. When I looked up she stood there with the child in her arms. She smiled. 'I had to give your son a bath, Mrs Ashcroft. He's such a greedy boy. He takes his feed too fast. He often throws up.'

I considered her words. I tried them out against my teeth. 'I have a son, he's a greedy boy.' It sounded all right. It sounded surprisingly good. I reached out.

'Give him to me please.'

Concern flickered in her face.

'It's all right, don't worry. I won't hurt him. I would never hurt him. Please leave us alone.'

When she'd gone I took him to Tessa's bed. It still smelled faintly of her perfume, the chemicals they used on her legs, humbugs. She loved humbugs.

Gently I took off his gown and his nappy. I laid him across my knees and looked at him for the first time. I liked the way his little purple feet turned in. I turned him on to his tummy and watched his back pulsing with his quick breathing. I ran my hand up his spine and his skin wrinkled beneath my fingers, rubbery like a puppy's belly. His breathing slowed for a moment and our bodies rose and fell together. I turned him again and he nuzzled against my breast even though the milk had dried up.

I bent my head over him. 'Welcome, Liam,' I whispered. 'This is your new birthday. The first day of your life for me.' I pressed my face into his hair. He smelled of sweat and strawberries.

I sang softly, 'Sweet, sweet you are. Nice enough to eat you are.' I drew him down into Tessa's bed. I felt his tiny penis stiffen against my leg, a warm spurt of urine dribbled over my thigh into the sheet. I laughed and rocked him. I saw them for a moment gathered around the bed. Tessa, Sadie, Doris, Betty, Gina, Mrs Pickering, Mrs Nisbet, Mavis, Cora, Evelyn. They raised a cheer for me. I was

BRAIN CANCER
Jenny Turner

Angela was really not sure what she was up to. The others were suspicious, that was for certain. But she was taking things fairly much in her stride. What else could she do? She was on an up.

The girls were all giggling in the cloakroom, having a smoke. They always did this first thing on a night out. Heather and Dee shared a packet of ten; Angela had her own because she stole them from her mum. They checked each other's liner smudge, back views and so on. Brain cancer, somebody said. The name of a boy. 'He was walking down Union Street and he seen us. He says Marlboros give you brain cancer. He's gorgeous, isn't he, Dee.'

'Oh that's it is it.'

In the dungeon they were lined up against a wall in the corridor as per usual and moving from the snakebites to rum and black. The rum had been Angela's idea. It was what her mother drank. It was something a bit different. Some boys got them. They hardly ever had to get their own. 'You want a drink?' a person would ask. 'Aye, but hold on, we'll give you the money,' they would reply, but while raking round their purses and pooling pennies and half ps the person got fed up of waiting. 'Look what do you want, I'll just go up to the bar now I think.' 'Och, never mind the now, I'll get it later.' Quite a few of them had jobs in any case. 'Oh, thanks a lot, hold on, I'll get you the money for it.' 'Och, dinna.' 'But I canna buy you one back. I canna get into buying rounds. I canna afford it.' 'Och, don't bother, look, here you go.' Hey Brain Cancer. He'd just come in, was being hailed by his mates. He was quite a little lad and had curly short hair, protruberant eyes, sunken cheeks and big, twisted teeth. He'd been in Germany the last six months, trying to make some money. It was well-known, he'd been a bit of a drinker before he went.

'Isn't he HANDSOME!!!!'

'Aye,' Angela agreed. He was, very.

She was feeling really good about herself. She lit one fag from the other. Talking to Brain Cancer. 'My mates call you Brain Cancer,' she said. 'Not very nice, eh,' he replied.

'You said if you smoke Marlboros you get brain cancer.'

'Never did did I?'

'You smoke Marlboros yourself, eh?'

'Is that you offering to crash the ash?'

He was a bit of a cut above. He wore plain black clothes, trousers, a T-shirt, boots, black harrington, which was okay. He was a bit older maybe? Maybe twenty or so. Not bad that. Just exactly right, in fact. He also managed a band, was the word. As they chatted on, Angela could half see the mates, at the other end of the corridor well into some other conversation. There might be consequences to this. What she was doing was breaking ranks.

She was especially aware of Dee, bobbing about in the vicinity of some boy Angela did not recognize. She was looking over as often as she dared, and without catching Angela's eye. Dee was worried and telling herself she could have nothing to worry about. Things are seldom as they look they are. Because it looked like he was responding to Angela when that could not, in fact, be the case. This was what she was hoping. Brain Cancer, or Paul as was his real name, had been Dee's project really. Well tough. Angela put her mind to the matter at hand.

'You're managing that band, eh?'

'Aye. I'm their official manager,' he replied.

'What's that mean you do then?'

'Not a lot. We've not got a lot in the way of gigs, ken.'

'Eh, but you're playing over Kaimhill next week, though.'

'Nobody's told ME nothing about it!!!'

'Heh, maybe they don't need a manager then.' The joke

was lost on Paul. 'Aye, maybe they don't,' he sighed. 'Used to play the bass and all with them, ken? Before I went away,' he said. 'Was it your idea they're called the Adaptorz?' Angela tried again. 'Nah,' was all he said.

'Silly name, isn't it?'

'It's all right.'

'What's it mean then?'

'Dah, ken.'

'What're they like anyway? Are they any good, even?'

'They're all right – you should come and see them, eh?'

'Hey, could I maybe get to see a practice sometime maybe?'

'Aye, if I can find out when they're on. Maybe they're telling me NOTHING, regarding rehearsals as well, heh?'

She got off with him somehow. What she did was, she dropped against him suddenly like she was tired and it worked. It was dark and so noisy in the corridor, nobody saw. 'Get me up to the hall in a minute,' he whispered. Right into one of her ears. So she let him go off and leaned flat against the wall. It was packed. She could not see Dee or Heather now, but some other people were about. She smiled and made faces. A guy came out of the men's toilet opposite with half his face opened. It was Lesbo the dealer: this meant big upheavals outside later. Paul was not the type to be much into fighting? Better not be. Better still: keep him out the way of it, and get him off up the road before the havoc began in earnest.

Her mates, she saw, were down the other end of the bar, all What-The-Fuck-Oh-No-Poor-Thing-But-He-Said-Aye-But-Ken-This-But-What's-REALLY-ON-The-Cards-Is-This about the brewing conflict. She might as well be off, good riddance. She did not feel like being a moll. So often you ended up just hanging about and watching it and talking about it. But now she had a man. Or nearly almost, she thought. Hee hee. On the way upstairs she had to push past a crowd of guys outside the men's then about tripped over Adam and George lying against the wall. 'What do you say if you're not saying glue?' they asked. They were taking their toll. 'Yoo hoo,' Angela said. 'Okay darling, you can pass,' Adam and George said, shifting their legs, with a grudge, but as she had answered correctly there was nothing they could do about it.

Up in the hall she saw Paul and took a breath. She went over to where he was sitting at the side of the dancing and sat down beside him. 'Hiya,' he said, turning to her and grinning. The sides of his eyes disappeared into lines as his mouth opened wide. 'Hiya,' he nestled – he made it very easy. She just fell on to his shoulder. It was a pose more suited to drastic occasions like after all battles are over and embraces well-deserved, but still. 'Hiya,' he said again and touched his cheek along her chin. Her jaw followed it a minute. It was slightly rough. Because he had been there longer than her, he was more slumped in his seat. This made her taller than him, and meant she had to take the lead really. She put her nearest arm over his shoulder as if they had been together through thick and thin and were now taking a moment off to look out to sea. He put his head on her shoulder and his nearest arm over to catch her other hand in his lap. As if it all was true. In a way it was. There was a chase and fighting and all. But down the stair, and Paul did not know about it. She wondered about mentioning it. Then decided not to. She did not find it interesting for it's own sake, fighting. Neither did she feel like making a show of interest for the sake of the others. It was their problem. She was keen to escape any hassle, and absolutely to keep Paul well out of it.

They sat there for quite a while, Angela wondering if this holding of him was enough. Then Paul poked his head up and said something. She didn't hear it. The disco was loud and she kind of liked the song. He said it again, lifting his head up so he could get right inside the ear.

'Not got a lad then?'
'No,' she said, then worried, 'Why have you?'
'Heh, got a lad.'
'Nah, you know fine what I mean,' in a cross voice. This he liked and laughed.

'Nah, I'm not going with anybody else.'

He was patting the top of her hand so she stroked at his curls. He turned again and said, 'You all right up there?'

'I'm just a bitty tired, is all.'

'Want to go up the road?'

'Aye, I wouldn't mind,' so off they went.

They were hand in hand which felt just fine. They did not run into any of Angela's mates or Paul's which was all for the best. They had to get down two flights of stairs full of punters, then across the lobby, which was lit always with fluorescent lights. The bouncers would be bound to see them then. Angela wondered what they would think. They must know her by now. She was there every week, often two times. It was the only place the mum didn't mind her going too much. 'You not got a late ticket then,' she asked Paul. 'Nah,' he said. 'I did,' she said. 'You want to stay then. We could sit in the wee lounge.' 'Nah,' she said, 'let's go.'

There was a couple of policemen at the porters' box. As they crossed the lobby, a scuffle came and Lesbo the dealer passed between two uniformed bouncers. He was being slung out. And probably worse, now that the police had arrived. He had blood on his face and his T-shirt was soaked down the front. He spotted them. 'Hey-yay Paulo!' he called as he was frogmarched past. 'Like Lesbo,' said Paul, and they stood there hand in hand another couple of minutes waiting for him to get well slung out. The policemen followed; so, yes, they were picking him up. Still hand in hand.

'A good mate of yours is he?' Angela asked.

'Aye, yes, the best. We was at school together. He bides just up the road from me.'

'So, why is he so mental then?'

'Lesbo cannot hold a drink. He likes a laugh and he cannot handle it once it gets started.'

69

'Oh, aye, can't handle his drink,' said Angela with sarcasm. 'So what about the drugs then?'

'For Lesbo the drugs are just a sideline,' Paul said. 'Sadly, this cannot also be said for some other of my good friends.'

He fell silent and was a bit upset: Angela hoped not because of her questions. The sound of a police van driving away came through the open door. Paul snapped out of his mood and said, 'But fuck me, aye, he's a wild one that Lesbo.' He chuckled.

'If you're such great mates, then, why're you not wild like him?'

'Heh, I, you see, can hold my drink,' Paul said. 'Very well indeed. And besides, I'm just not a wild sort of a person.' He turned round and kissed her, bang on the mouth, there, right in the middle of the lobby. She gave him a little push so they could get moving and OUT, out of the building and the bright light at least.

They were both of them well bleezing. This they realized the minute they got out in the fresh air. Angela was hard put to see straight so she let her eyes relax. So all was fuzzy and she could not see far. 'Want chips?' said Paul. 'Nah,' she said. 'You go ahead I'll wait for you.' 'Nah, won't bother,' Paul said, though she could tell he was gasping. Instead he lit up a cigarette. After a draw he passed it to her. 'Heh, Marlboro,' she said. 'Heh, brain cancer.'

Angela did not live far away. It was twenty minutes maybe. A lot longer though, if you are away with it and staggering. Paul snorkeled a lot and was half falling over. Which Angela liked, because he fell on to her. He was a head taller or so than her, quite wee really. She put both arms around him, one round the front, the other along the back so her hands met and clasped each other round the far side. He was cold in his thin jacket, nearly shivering. It was March and a cold night for it.

At the corner was a boutique which sold denims and things and had a second-hand record mart up the back. 'Hey look,' Angela said, as she stared into the window of the shop. 'What?' Paul said, coming up behind her and laying his head chin first upon her shoulder.

'Nothing,' she said with a snorkel, letting herself fall backwards.

'Hey, yay, sweet nothing,' he quoted, and snorkeled too.

'Nice top that dear one,' she said eventually. 'You buy it for me, eh? As a token of your great esteem.'

'Some chance, wish I could.'

'They've got some really nice stuff in there, you ever go in? If only I'd the money, shite.'

'I really like what you've got on,' Paul said sounding injured. 'I think you've got really nice dress sense. It's a really nice dress.'

'I made the dress myself actually.'

'Fuck! Howdy manage that!'

'My mum showed me how to do dressmaking.'

'Wow,' he said with a funny roll of the eyes, 'WOW. I wish my mum could show me things like that!'

'Anyhow, I think you've got really nice gear yourself,' she said. Both the last contributions were stupid. But they were drunk and enjoying it and testing each other out a little.

Just by the top of Angela's road was a lane in which they were putting up new houses for the elderly. In front of the building site was a wall and a little park bench for some reason. They sat there a bit and again she was giggling. The cold probably had a lot to do with it. But she liked the bit about him liking her clothes. She thought he thought she was strange and new. It was getting colder but they sat there talking about this and that. And petting, and then she felt his hand touch her pants. 'Hey, dinna,' she said. He nipped it away. 'Sorry, but I can handle it, honest,' he said. 'Aye, but you think I can?' so it was all passed in a sophisticated manner. In case Paul was aggrieved she gave him a huge and gasping cuddle and asked if he'd be down at the beach the morn. 'Aye,' he said, 'if you want me to be.'

'You think I'm nice, eh?'

'You're really nice.' Buried in her front he sounded choked.

'So why d'y like me so much, eh?'

Fuck. Angela's mother was suddenly appeared round the corner. Arms crossed on the chest and she was taking short fast steps. She was in a complete panic. Her baby girl where could she be. 'My mum,' Angela hissed, and Paul stood up. He held out a hand and helped her to her feet. They walked over to the mother and Angela said, 'Hi mum, how d'y know I was here?' 'I didn't,' the mum said. 'This is the third time I've been out looking for you.'

'This is Paul, mum. We were talking.'

'Hello, Paul,' she said.

'Hello, Angela's mum,' Paul said, then with a click of the head, 'Must be going,' and off he went. Hands in his trouser pockets, head hunched over from the cold. From what he had been saying, he still had a good two or three miles to walk on up the hill.

The next afternoon Angela turned up at the beach, like most weeks, with the dog. She couldn't get out of it, she said. In fact, she really liked the dog and was glad to have it along. Some of the lads made a fuss of it and it got a good run, sticks thrown and so on. Angela suspected the dog showed her to advantage. Heather sometimes took hers along, a yappy little cairn. Though not lately come to think on it. She hadn't turned up yet. Just a bunch of the usual boys.

Paul was sitting, unlike the rest of the squad, in T-shirt only. It wasn't that warm. He did not seem perturbed to see Angela approach him smiling. He grinned and held up a hand from where he was lying, flat up in the lee of a wave barrier. The dog jumped on him and started licking away like mad. He laughed and gave it a rub. 'Thon mutt doesn't go for boys much,' she said to him. 'You're in luck. If any come to our door it goes mental and tries to bite their legs off.' 'We'll see what it does when I start coming round, eh Ange?' he said. His arms were tight and brownish. It looked like being a lovely body actually, but awful cold. Angela had a huge sweatshirt and a coat on and had no intention whatever of taking even the latter off. 'You not freezing,' she asked, not daring to look anywhere near him. 'You're all coming out in goose pimples. All down your arms see.'

'Aye, right as ever, Ange,' he said, and sat up to get his jumper and jacket back on. The dog sat staring at him, waiting for him to notice it had placed a piece of wood right at his feet.

Once he'd organized himself Angela sat herself in about Paul's waist. Heather and Dee appeared off the bus and passed her a dirty look. 'Oh, aye,' they said. 'Like, I brought the dog along,' Angela said. Some lads were goading it with its stick. No sooner said than it was halfway up the beach all yelps of total delight. 'So you got in all right last night?' said Heather. 'We were thinking of phoning your mum to see what had happened to you.'

'Hiya, girls,' said Paul. 'Fit like?'

'No bad, Paul, fit like yourself,' Heather said. Dee only managing a thin and mean looking smile and a single sound.

'So you're the quineys that give me a bad name.'

They had not a clue what he meant and looked offended. 'Brain Cancer,' he said and they giggled and Dee tried to explain. The two mates muttered something then went up to the caff for cones. They were laughing and leaning into each other as they went. Dee had new shorts on and long socks. She'd been talking about them last night, Angela remembered. In the toilets.

Paul and her had a snog then stopped. The dog returned and jumped on top. 'Aye, aye, Paul,' said a voice. 'Here's Steve,' said Paul sounding pleased. It was Steve and he was with Fiona. This was better. Fiona did not know what had been going on and just said, 'Fit like Angela,' with a laughing look. 'We was just going up the caff,' said Steve.

'Fancy it?' said Paul, so they followed them up. 'Steve's my best mate,' he added.

'Thought Lesbo was your best mate, you said,' said Angela.

'Nah, not really. Not any more,' said Paul.

'Fiona's about my best mate now, ken.'

'I've not met her before,' said Paul. 'So is she going about with Steve then?'

'A couple of weeks,' said Angela, and running caught up with Fiona, who said, 'So that's what happens when I dinna come out with youse eh, and where's the rest of the squad?'

In the caff the dog was knackered, so well-behaved under the table. Dee and Heather were cheered up, slipping the dog spare chips from each other's plates, when they thought nobody was looking. Then some of the guys came in and started taking the rib about the UHU joke. 'The boy, the boy, he had a tube up each fucking nostril man.' 'Don't sniff glue, sniff Yoo Hoo.' 'Oy, sunny, what you wanting with that crisp bag?' and the like. Talk got on to what happened last night. And what was going on with Lesbo, the dealer, in general.

'What'll his ma and da say?'

'What a fucking head case.'

'Aye, and Donald was in there too, they've lifted him and all.'

'NOT Donald Schmonald?' says Dee.

'Aye, it was trouble about DRUGS.'

'NOT DRUGS,' they all yelled, then thought the better of it, it being a humble and respectable family run seaside caff.

The next week Paul rang up and asked Angela out, a proper date he said. There was a show of Oor Wullie on at the theatre. Paul was dead into Oor Wullie. 'He'd got the tickets and everything, he said.' 'Maybe you can have him in for coffee after,' the mum said as Angela was leaving. 'Can't we sit in my room and listen to records?' Angela said. 'You can't sit in a room with a boy, not a bedroom, not on your nelly,' the mum replied.

Paul got her a vodka in the interval so her breath wouldn't smell. He had every single Oor Wullie annual from 1968 on he said. He said she should get a pair of them baggy dungarees. With her haircut she would look swell. 'I'll get you a bucket for your birthday,' he said. When they got back to the house, in the lounge Angela's wee brother was full out on the mat, pyjamas half-falling off of him. The mother was hard at work trying to pick at his verruca, as had to be done every night before bed. Angela was black affronted. Conversation was tense. It stuck strictly to what had happened in the show. 'Was Soapy in it?' asked the mum. 'What about Wee Eck? What was the scenery like? Oh him, wasn't he in something on the TV?' Then the brother chipped in with, was Paul growing a moustache? And if so, what was it like and how long did it take? Angela could not wait for Paul to leave. When he did, the mum said, 'What a nice young lad. Awful quiet though, isn't he?'

'He's very shy mum,' Angela said, and went through to her room and sat listening to some disc for hours.

Then Paul rang up and caught her in during the day. She only skived for certain periods of certain days. It depended on the teacher and other things. She usually bunked off, then sat at home by the fire eating biscuits and watching For Schools And Colleges TV.

'I got the day off work,' he said.

'How come?'

'Took it off, didn't I? Listen my mum's out so you can come up if you like.'

'Aye and what for?'

'Oh, I dah ken. Sit on the couch. Watch TV. She's out till teatime. Honestly Ange.'

'Och, no, I don't fancy it,' she said. 'Anyhow I've not got a clue where it is you stay.'

'I'll get you from the bus stop, eh?'

'Nah, nah, Paul. I better be back for the afternoon. Honest I'd better.'

'Och. See you Friday then, eh?'

'Sure thing, aye. See you Friday.'

Friday was not so bad. There was a band up in the hall that Dee and Heather raved about. Angela though thought she'd better sit downstairs in the bar with Paul. A lot of his mates were about. 'So what the fuck I might be an alky,' he was saying. 'So what the fuck I happen to like my drink. You dinna really notice it, do you? You still like me fine, eh?'

'So why not not drink so much then,' said Angela. What a joke. Every time he went out more or less, it had to be where the mates were going. Then they all just got bleezing. Angela liked them all fine. She liked being around when they were bleezing, even. The crack was good. But being attached to one of them, who slobbed over his words and kept giving her sentimental looks, was different. Or so she sometimes thought.

'I'm getting it Ange, so what'll you have?'

'You're guttered Paul, you're guttered.'

'Och, but you still like me fine, eh? You still like me fine. Ken?'

'Ken, I like you fine, fine, FINE, eh. Eh, like, Adam.'

'Yaroo,' Adam said politely, sitting himself down. 'Drink? DRINK? What a sin! Me, I'm into speed, that's S.P.E.E.E.D., the active person's drug for the active person's life style.'

'No, I'm not into it. I'm not into that at all,' said Paul. He raised himself on to his hands with difficulty. 'No, no, I'm no into drugs at all. I'm off to the bar. What can I get you? A coke is it, eh Ange?' Angela wondered. Adam and Paul were pretty good mates. They hung about a lot together. Adam had an eye on Dee but Dee was not keen. Angela told her she was daft. He had a load of personality had Adam. But yes, he was into drugs and he was well fucked up.

'Hn hn hn, aw shite, I love the way you kiss,' gasped Paul as they said goodnight on the corner.

'Mm hm,' Angela snuggled. She was feeling better about things now. She kissed him again, very hard.

'Fucksake, who taught you to do THAT?!!'

'My mum did!' she giggled. 'You should know!! You should know by now!!! She taught me EVERYTHING I KNOW!!!!'

'I really like you Ange? I really really like you? You know that, eh? We're a right pair, eh? A right pair?'

'Hey Paul, man, the time. I better be getting in or it'll be mum out on the streets again, heh?'

'Tartan skirt and bitching specs. Verrucay cream and all, aye.'

'Heheh. Aw. Awfuck. Awfuck.'

Angela stood a minute and watched him lurch to the side of the road. His hands to the mouth. Sure enough he started honking up into the gutter. It sounded sore. He'd be embarrassed. She stood on for a minute or two. Then called, 'Hey Paul, that's me off in,' and ran down the road, leaving him to get on with it.

Saturday always was a comedown after Fridays. There was no late licence and not much cash left either. Angela met Paul for a quiet drink as arranged. Some others wandered in to play on the machines mostly. Like Paul, they said and sat down. They were getting a bus organized to Glasgow to see some band. Adam was dealing with it. 'You fancy it any of youse?' Adam said. He seemed completely straight now. 'Dah ken,' said Paul, 'what about it Angie?' 'Aye, what about it Angie?' Adam said. 'Good laugh. Heaps o beer. Heaps o boys. Boys in heaps, eh.'

'I'd be dead into it,' Angela said, then fell silent. The chat went on around her. Paul was drinking fast on pints others were buying for him. His money was all finished. He'd not be able to get his round. He wasn't saying much either.

They didn't say much on the way up the road that night. Till just over halfway, when Angela stopped and said, 'I think we'd better just call it a day, don't you?' 'What, eh?' he said. 'Why? What for?' 'I can't handle getting serious,' she said. 'I think you're too old for me. Anyhow you drink too much. You're bleezing every night.'

'Still be mates, eh?'

'Still be mates.' He looked like he was crying as he wandered away. All hunched up as usual. Again it was cold. It had been all of three weeks, Angela's longest to date. That was probably why it felt like an awful lot longer.

SPRING MORNING WITH ALP

Drummond Bone

Alp looked up at Professor Weddle. Professor Weddle looked down at Alp. The dog's labrador blackness was labrador grey around the muzzle. Professor Emeritus Weddle sympathized. This sympathy took the form of a bag of Winalot biscuits, a portion of which was Alp's version of the 'bird seed' – not Alpen – which Weddle would shortly pour out for his own breakfast. The sympathy was not a product of the early spring sun, but an enduring matutinal understanding of quite a few years. Weddle reflected that he had forgotten when Alp went grey, and had indeed more or less forgotten how long Alp had been with him. Both things seemed to have happened gradually, like his own ageing, though he could remember the cardboard box in which Alp had travelled to their house for the first time – for what seemed like years it had lain in a pile of other cardboard boxes on the concrete floor of the old wash-house. The Winalot bag was hoisted not without effort back to its safely high shelf. Weddle turned round again to look at the dog, who was now snuffily preoccupied – of course – with the few biscuits still left in his bowl. When Alp's box had been in the pile of Robinson's or Lurpak or Crosse & Blackwell cartons in which they had carried their groceries home from town – then they had shopped in a *proper* grocer's, with now old-fashioned wooden shelving, drawers with enamel name-plates for spices and herbs, and everything wrapped in brown paper with impossible neatness – then, well then it had been 'they'. Nowadays he only went to that shop for what he now, and then they, called his 'bird-seed'. For the rest, the temptation of Tesco's car park won hands down. Weddle rubbed his fingers carefully around the bowl that Alp drank from, washing away the remains of yesterday's enthusiastic licking with what he was aware was over-careful deliberation. He filled the bowl and steered it to the floor past Alp's pressing enthusiasm. And, as an afterthought, patted and scratched the bowed head as it lapped. Then he washed his hands and started to assemble his own breakfast.

Although breakfast was not an elaborate meal, he took it in the dining room, at the head of the table. This meant a multiple journeying from the kitchen, for Weddle was constitutionally incapable of using a tray. The effort of loading and unloading seemed to him infinitely more work than the three trips it took to carry plate and spoon, milk and cup, and lastly teapot – though the whole enterprise had, he admitted every morning, a certain dottiness. All the more eccentric too as he ate his evening meal, which he sometimes took considerable pains over, he prided himself – most mornings and most evenings – he ate that in the lounge by the side of the fire, if he lit the fire that is, for often the central heating now seemed enough. This was so much his custom that reading material was allotted accordingly.

On the dining-room table were the latest journals, always out of their wrappers but perhaps not always read, with the exception of *Nature* and *Scientific American* which he always read, never quite without the suspicion that he found the photographic illustrations a comfort. On the other hand he rarely descended to *New Scientist*, and that he did find comforting. Whatever, his place at the head of the table might well have been conditioned by the teetering piles of scientific wisdom and research. By his chair at the fireside however a novel – Thackeray or Trollope perhaps, James if he was feeling strong, Bennett or Buchan if he was particularly limp. There, too, there was an accumulation of material, from time to time regrouped after Alp had been through it in his own way, but it was only rarely that a novel got carried to the dining room, or a journal or magazine to the lounge. Alp, he was pleased to feel, was at home in both rooms, even if he organized his presence by morning or evening to follow his master's.

This morning the sun cut across the right-hand side of the window, the dining room was light, and later it would be warm. Meantime, one bar of the electric fire was a help. Weddle turned the pages of an article on fractals, with a disapproval which had as much to do with his daily disappointment that he could no longer drink coffee – or was *told* that he no longer *should* – as it was to do with his desire to believe that what he was reading was all rubbish. He knew that it wasn't, but wished that it were. Alp appeared by his side, and insinuated his head under his armpit, between arm and table. Weddle absent-mindedly joggled it in friendly fashion with his elbow, and Alp grumbled appreciation. Infinite lines within finite spaces – Weddle thought with a snarl – could we fit one inside your head, my old chap? Oh, it's getting beyond us, I fear. It's not instinctive any more. But he was still in front of the article a good hour later, and though the sun was now actually beginning to warm his right side, the bar-fire was still singing on his left, and even Alp had found it too hot, and had retreated under the table.

On the third return trip from dining room to kitchen, this time with cup and teapot, Weddle found himself thinking both about arriving at Harderode in an army lorry in 1945 – the colour of the tiles on a mansard roof just at the moment when on a sunny June day he jumped down from the front seat – and about Julia Weddle carrying a teapot in the reverse direction to himself at this minute, on what could have been one of thousands of days. The touch of wonder at the oddity of the conjunction he felt as if it were Alp trying to squeeze past him through the kitchen doorway – but in his second's pause, he discovered that Alp wasn't there at all. A barely audible adjustment of jaws told him that Alp was still where he had last seen him, under the table. So what had he thought? He put the teapot down carefully, trying for no reason except the satisfaction not to make a sound, and stood with his left hand holding the white cup by its matching saucer while he tried to refocus the two overlapping memories. But now all he could catch was a smell and then an accompanying composition of field kitchen, huge barrel-like stoves, slanting pipes for flues – three of them, one for each stove, and roped together with guys against the wind – standing on brick props alongside a walkway of broken planks and old doors . . . this was behind the row of houses with the mansard roofs, he knew, but could not really picture their spatial relationship. Then as he remembered the cup he remembered Julia standing as he now stood, not holding a cup and saucer in this ridiculous still life, to be sure, but at the sink as he was, in fact in exactly the same place as he now was, occupying the same planes, the same angles, and curiously the same time. Only, not even Julia could have remembered the field kitchen at Harderode. The saucer had reached the surface of the draining board, and Weddle removed his fingers from its edge. Through the kitchen window, by leaning slightly forward and looking sharply to his left he could see that the lime tree was not yet in leaf. But it would only be a few more days.

This was the moment of the day in which to draw up the shopping list, and Weddle cast around the kitchen table and the shelves above it to find the elusive pencil. Then he paused. To whom really did the battered stoves belong, the knots that held the hot ropes around the flues, the panelled door that bent over the muddy dip in the path as he walked along – where to? Was it really green paint delaminating from the wood? It all almost seemed his sole property as he remembered it. But was it? No one else to lay a claim. The pencil appeared actually to have vanished, but Weddle resignedly knew that it would be there – somewhere – tomorrow. It came and went with a will of its own. There was a pen in his jacket, but his jacket was hanging in the hall, and he was reluctant to fetch the pen from it, and then have to return after he had finished his list to put the jacket on to go out. And to turn two separate tasks into one by simply fetching the jacket was somehow an admission that the pencil had defeated him. Well, he thought, it's too good a morning to miss – a brief stroll round the garden, then we'll see about the shopping. There was no need to call Alp, who appeared, of course, quicker than Weddle's thought. He let Alp out of the door first, to avoid an unseemly bustling dispute. To allow to go first – he framed the sentence to himself without a clear understanding of any context, though in the space between deciding first to close the door and therefore to check that he had his housekey, and then deciding not to close it at all but to let in – as he put it – the spring air, in this withdrawn movement of his arm he was puzzled by the idea of sequence: arriving at Harderode, Julia, Alp. He shut the door and suddenly jumped as he realized he had not felt for his key after all. But it was there, in his hip-pocket, as always, nevertheless.

Underneath the lime tree all the snowdrops had disappeared some time ago, but a few aconites struggled on in the longer days and the increasing heat. In their outer band the daffodils themselves had seen better days. Alp was off sniffling back and forwards along the base of the back wall. No doubt there was a timely order to things there too, though Weddle had no notion of what it might be. Alp had tormented everything from field mice to rabbits to frogs, at what seemed like characteristic seasons, though that may have been only Weddle's fancy. The article on fractals made him examine the bark on the lime tree, in a vague way tracing the gulfs and gulleys in search of repeated shape. The surface of the tree, however, seemed to have less of a three-dimensional quality, or less of a multi-dimensional quality, than the mono-dimensional representations of multi-dimensionality on his Apple II (a recent retirement present to himself – there had been, he was guiltily conscious, a whole series of retirement 'presents' now reaching the levels of the absurd). This flattening of the world's complexity struck him, as he stood there suspiciously eyeing the tree, as very much odder than his madly blossoming complexity of programme or theory. For all his scepticism of chaos theory that was more the way things surely had to be . . . rather than this faintly bewildering simplicity in front of him. It was the dimension of time that was missing, of course, he thought, and he patted the tree in friendly forgiveness. For the computer compressed time, and generated its chaotic orders, its infinities within finites, in a visible time that was quite unknown in the world as perceived. Under his hand, as he thought, the tree began to feel rough, then at once his fingers slid into the folds of the bark, its ridges sharp yet crumbling on his palm, and he found that he had been standing in such an uncomfortable position, leaning forward, that all his weight was being supported by his outstretched arm. With difficulty he pushed himself vertical, the bark imprinted on his hand. Where was Alp? How long had this tree taken to grow? It comfortably outreached the house – one hundred, two hundred, years? Under the influence not only of its genetic code, as it were, but under the countless, countless, daily variations of temperature and wind and humidity, and yet on its own scale predictable. He thought he heard the sounds of parting grass behind the yew hedge, and walked around it, half expecting to be knocked into by the dog . . . but Alp wasn't there. Weddle walked on round to the front of the house, and measured the blueness of the sky beyond the trees.

Although he had almost called Alp, he had not, but had made a little decision to face a sense of Julia's absence privately, for a second or two. It never lasted more than a second or two in any case, for then she would return quite happily to his mind, standing beside him now as he looked down at the primroses which suggested a sort of boundary between the lawn that was barely not meadow, and the line of beech trees that themselves defined in some manner his land from the fields beyond. They had not planted the primroses, he knew, and wondered as he had wondered every spring whether someone else had, or if they had just one year started to appear, some kind of Easter magic. There had been a time, easy to say, when he had simply not known Julia – there had been a time after all when he had not yet known Harderode and its red-tiled houses and its field kitchen – and why should this seem now so unreasonable when absolutely no one in Harderode would have known him before he got there in 1945, nor would know him now, or even remember him then, or possibly even remember the field kitchen which had come back to him so vividly this morning? Even Julia did not know him then, and did not know his *now* then, nor could know it now, *this* now. Well, of course you couldn't, he said aloud to his memory beside him. Of course you couldn't. But that's not the point. Weddle would have been hard put to say what was the point, however.

He looked down at the primroses, and gradually he found himself looking down at one primrose. He sighed, not unpleasantly. Something was crashing about in the undergrowth – it might have been the dog, but it might only have been a blackbird, it was so difficult to guess the size of unseen commotion. Weddle had often speculated that he couldn't tell an elephant from a rabbit, supposing an elephant could have been hidden in his rhododendrons. And this primrose. A symmetrical study in the finest transformations of delicate colour, too spectral to be only green or even primrose yellow. Weddle pondered the bark and the plant that was now under his absent-looking gaze. The colour seemed closer to the fractal curves that explained its own generation than did the three-dimensional bark of the lime tree, while the simplicity of the petals was a simple symmetry, an order that needed no computer to prove it to the eye. What was it about the colour though? The fact that its seeming mono-dimensionality was an illusion, and that the mind knew it to be an illusion, was already working in a whole complex of changing prismatic effects of light and texture? But that would be true too of the bark, which after all was not monochrome, had its own shades and tones and colours? But less obviously perhaps, less obviously to the point that the mind rejected that sense as insignificant. Whereas the primrose . . . without the colour, what of its symmetry? Oh this beautiful bloom of a few spring weeks!

Weddle stood looking down for a good minute or two, though perhaps it seemed even longer to him. The flower was beautiful, he knew, but this loving attempt to find its beauty in his own terms was telling him something new. Its beauty was somehow no longer his concern. There it was, this marvel, and he was quite happy to use the word marvel or the word wonder – he had never been ashamed of such words – with Julia or indeed with anyone, but it wasn't any more his concern. Or it lay in his mind in the same way as the glowing angled roofs of the occupied village, or as Julia's hand in his. He sighed again. He rubbed his hand where he could still feel the imprint of the lime-tree bark. Time had passed. Alp he knew was somewhere, and he would come if he called.

FROM A MOTH-EATEN ETHNOGRAPHICAL MANUSCRIPT

Frank Kuppner

1.

The Maya capital, notorious for . . . a large central plain . . . dotted by numerous . . .
 . . . in the reign of Anáhualtec, whose right hand . . . to the obvious disbelief of . . .
 . . . under that archway the curiously warm-eyed maidens used to gather, looking at each other with the utmost contempt . . . who lived very close by, and whose sceptres of office, protruding through the windows, glinted in the morning sun . . . which surprised them greatly . . . so that murmuring they said: . . .
He replied: 'I am Farahuada, come here from a far land: to bring you these benefits . . . into the constellations . . . gold smelting . . . nuclear fission . . . the enchanting counterpoint of . . .
'I would prefer that little one over there . . . all this pointless business . . . what exactly do you mean . . . male and female . . .'
And the noise which the jade pendants made rustling against their throats and ankles was tumultuous. 'Stay!' they shouted. 'Do not leave us!' Until a voice from among the assembled crowd . . . they are a lot nicer than they must seem from where you are standing, my . . . but that is quite unnecessary . . . We must bring news of this to Chichén-Itzá before the sun sets.
Joy settled among the villages like . . .

One hundred thousand virgins were led out on to a long ramp in front of the rising sun. And the chief priest, gripped by unusual emotion . . . but the clouds soon lifted . . . emerging at length from behind the altar . . .

They fell to the ground, howling. None . . .

'I have come to put an end to this,' Vonoda yelled. 'It is utterly inconceivable that even now, in this day and age . . .'

In the end they managed to persuade her to turn and face in the opposite direction.

2.

'And that?' Vonodo asked, pointing to the girl's navel.

3.

The old temples were destroyed, the old statues cast down. The priests of the old religion took to hiding in the mountains.

'These people claim,' said Veindo, 'to come from over the seas, or from beyond the nearest sea. Are we so stupid that we must believe their claims? Gullible, yes. Gullible . . . Over the sea, men are of an entirely different colour, and the women, frankly, dress ridiculously.

But these newcomers do not even sleep.

They watch our sleeping children, and break into what they claim is not laughter . . . are not to be deceived so easily. We know what laughter is. We have been taught.

Ha, ha, ha . . . or this left hand . . .

. . . for it is better, ultimately, to call rain by its proper name.

. . . and as for the alfalfa . . .'

ETHNOGRAPHICAL MANUSCRIPT

4.

Vonodo was perhaps the kindest of the intruders, although his preferences . . . particularly . . . a little unusual, even for an extra-terrestrial . . . and only the fact that he was, for most of the time, invisible . . . which used to frustrate him horribly, and occasionally caused him to . . . but they were used to it . . . no choice but to agree to.

5.

'We came here hoping to educate you, to rescue you, but you are all too evidently not interested in that sort of thing. I don't understand how . . .
  'I remember when I myself was half your age . . . the swaying spheres . . . my mother's voice . . . the sheer cosmic normalcy of sexual disaster . . .'

6.

. . . following a running female deep into the tamarack forests on the off-chance that . . . the sunlight . . . inevitably . . .
  Until one day as he lay supine on the floor of the forest, trying to remember what grass was, and what he had been told about the deep caves which, so rumour has it . . . arriving and seeming at first . . . but at the very last moment changed her mind.
  This killed him. It also caused the death of . . .

7.

'Yes, ugly. And what can you possibly hope to gain by seeking to drop stone slabs upon our officials? How do you tally this with your supposed ancestor-worship? Really, I sometimes think, if it weren't for the cleavage . . .

We have met types long before now who were far more violent than you, far far more violent – you over-estimate yourselves – and whose technologies were such as to afford us what I think I can honestly call moments of lack of confidence. Who exactly do you think you are anyway? When our leader . . . no, not dead, and not missing either . . . not at the moment . . . frankly we prefer the space between the stars to the ridiculously steep stairways of which . . .

Be warned: you will regret this. It may already be too late . . . never forget about the sun . . .'

8.

Soon afterwards they held a great meeting in the main square underneath the magnetic fire-producer. Dogs vanished utterly.

They went from house to house . . . groaning . . . trying to install in each . . . which looked like a telephone . . . in unison.

With a supercilious giggle . . .

But their belief that children were produced by pressing a finger for a certain length of time against a woman's eye . . .

Some things cannot be disguised.

. . . since otherwise their existence seemed superfluous.

Or, perhaps, they only pretended to believe that.

9.

'. . . with the sole intention of helping you, of improving or mitigating your harsh existence in the bright sunlight, rescuing you from laughter and nudity, and what reward or gratitude do we receive in return?'

By wiring this to this it should certainly be possible . . .

'. . . certainly not our reason. But the sad truth is, you

prefer this life of brutal indolence. You do not even have enough wit to be envious of us, our crystalline facets . . . a particularly strong drink . . . reasonably big and responsive . . . stupor induced by setting alight . . . where every roof sprouts its battalions of aerials . . . don't talk to me about blondes . . . you would prefer . . . shambling raven-haired oaf.'

There must be, absolutely, millions . . .

'. . . look, for the last time, you stupid woman . . .'

'. . . spread everywhere . . . no, not you.'

10.

When the old king, whom many people had thought was dead, came down from the mountains at the head of an immense quantity of . . . virulent diseases . . . introduced deliberately.

For a full day battle raged somewhere or other, and, at the end of the day . . .

And the King said: 'I (or perhaps, He) . . .'

'. . . were bound hand and foot, and thrown inside the flaming compartments; and when we opened our eyes again all was still.'

Although lubricants . . .

'I remember,' someone said, 'when the town was exactly like this before.'

'. . . grief-stricken . . . on the ground . . .'

'. . . more women . . .'

'. . . which all of us who were there will never forget.'

III.

(*Sic. Possibly spurious? Perhaps a fragment of a different manuscript?*)

'. . . filled our homes . . . but for years we half-expected their return.'

Occasionally, in spring, a traveller just returned from a valley in the north . . .

'. . . and all would rush to the place, hoping to see some trace . . . but there was nothing.'

A broken twig or two, whose origin was almost certainly earthly . . .

Actually, it was only then that we realized that . . .

THE POSTER
Ken Ross

Alec said, 'Whit we need's a fuckin' big poster.'
   People said 'aye' and 'yeah'. Dougie said 'Whit for?'
'Tae hang, fer Christ's sake. Oot the windae.'
'*That* windae?'
'Ach, what windae d'ye think?'
From where they sat on the floor all they could see was sky. Joe levered himself to his feet, tripped over someone's legs and half-fell against the window ledge. He looked down twenty-two floors to the car park by the underground station, and the road, and beyond, further, to the long grey scarf of the river, and the city, and a switchback of motorway, and the green hills.
   'Ah mean, big,' said Alec. 'Big. So she'll bloody see.' He opened another can with his left hand and accepted the joint from Paddy with his right.
   'Fuckin' earwax, that, it's no' dope. It's no' dope, that, it's fuckin' earwax,' said Paddy, leaning back on his elbows. 'Fuckin' earwax, it is.'
   'Ach, come on,' said Stewart. 'Come on.'
   'Ah'm tellin' ye.'
   'Fuckin' Maryhill ah went tae fer that.'
   'Aye, well.'
   'She'll no' come by here,' said Dougie.
   'She's *comin'* by here,' said Alec. 'City chambers fuckin' reception, then aff tae the East End tae open a park or somethin'. Which way else she's gonnae come? Fuckin' procession. Fuckin' *car*. By *here*.'
   'Lob a bomb, ye could,' said Joe, looking out.
   'Ach sure, bombs. Ah'll just run doon tae the shop.'

'Stuck tae yer hand that?' said Stewart.

'A wee grenade – y'know?' Joe made a large bowling action with his arm. 'Wheeeee – splat. Mince.'

'Aye, right,' said Paddy.

'Ah said, is that stuck tae yer hand?'

'Fuckin' mince,' said Joe, leaning down to pick a can from the cardboard tray.

'Ach, sorry pal,' said Alec, having been nudged. He passed the joint on.

'Whit's that the number of yon can ye're havin' there?' said Dougie.

'Talkin' tae me, Dougie?' said Joe.

'Aye. Whit's like the load o' thae cans doon yer throat the day, eh?'

'Ach,' said Joe, ripping the ring away and pushing the vent to his mouth.

'Are we nigh oot?' said Paddy.

'Ach no,' said Alec, 'ach no.'

'Ah'm only sayin',' said Dougie, drinking moodily. There was a silence as the joint passed and arms rose and fell. Empties lay scattered around on the bare floor. That day's and the days' before. The afternoon sun slid from behind clouds and hit through the glass. The room was full for a moment with bright motes of smoke.

'Aitcheson Court Says No' said Alec, placing the words in the air with his hand. The others looked at him. 'On the *poster*, ah'm talkin' aboot the *poster* – "Aitcheson Court Says No" – big fuckin' letters.'

'"No"?'

'Aye, "No." "Aitcheson Court Says . . ."'

'Ah heard ye,' said Paddy. 'Ah heard ye.'

'That's pathetic, that,' said Dougie.

'No tae what?' said Joe.

'Tae . . . tae . . . her . . . tae . . . a' this . . . tae . . . aw fuck, just "no", y'know? "No tae what?" – Christ, man.'

'Pathetic,' said Dougie.

'Whit's wrang wi' it?' said Stewart.

'Whit's wrang wi' it?'

THE POSTER

'Aye.'

'Ah'll tell ye whit's wrang wi' it.'

'Aye, you tell me.'

'Ah will, ah'll tell ye.'

'Hoo's aboot – "Aitcheson Courts Says Fuck Off"?' said Joe. There was a long pause.

'Naw,' said Paddy, 'naw.'

'Ye've no class, you,' said Alec.

'Aye, it's no' right, that,' said Stewart. 'Fuck off's no' right.'

'Please yersels,' said Joe. He turned to the window again, tilting his can vertically to get the last dregs.

'Whit ah'm sayin' . . .' began Dougie. He was interrupted by Stewart, who had sucked violently on the last quarter inch of the joint and then doubled up with racking coughs.

'It's deid, that one,' said Paddy.

'Oh Christ, oh ma Christ,' said Stewart, whooping for air, his hand scrabbling for his can.

'Ye're aye greedy, son,' said Paddy. Stewart levered himself upright, pouring the beer down. 'Roll us anither one, fer Christ's sake.'

'An' it'd be . . .' said Alec, his eyes focused on the distance, 'it'd be forty-foot big, fifty foot, naw, mair than that, doon, right doon, a' the way tae the ground, an' right over, right across, ye wouldnae see the fuckin' block here at a', jest that, hangin' there, jest sayin' it, jest tellin' her. Ach, it'd be brilliant, man.' And there was a silence again, and they all looked into the distance and saw it, the huge poster the height of the tower.

'It'd be red,' said Paddy, quietly, 'bright fuckin' red.'

'Aye,' said Joe. 'Aye.'

'Naw,' said Dougie.

'Naw?'

'No. "Aitcheson Court" that's no' it.'

'Fer why no' Aitcheson Court? This *is* fuckin' Aitcheson Court,' said Paddy.

'Ach, use yer heids. Whit's it mean?'

'Mean?'

95

'Aye,' Dougie paused, pulled a can towards him, and opened it, deliberately, sure of his audience. He took a careful draught. 'Nothin' – that's whit it means. Tae her, ah'm sayin', tae her. Never fuckin' heard o' the place. Where's yer . . . whit's the word?'

'Impact,' said Stewart, his fingers busy crumbling brown dust the length of the next joint.

'Aye, right,' said Dougie. 'Where's yer impact?'

'Ye've got a poster the size o' a fuckin' tower-block and you're sayin' there's no impact?' said Alec. 'Ye're away wi' the wee men, son.'

'It disnae mean *nothin'*. Tae *her*, ah'm sayin', tae her. So . . .' Dougie smiled and took another swig. 'Ah'd have . . .' – he raised his arms in a dramatic sweep – 'The *Gorbals* Says No.'

They looked at it in their minds.

'Aye, well,' said Stewart, lighting up, 'she'll ha' heard o' the Gorbals right enough.'

'Right enough,' said Paddy. 'D'ye no' think, Alec?'

'Ach, it's a' right,' said Alec.

'A' right?' said Dougie. 'A' right?'

Joe fell off the windowsill on which he'd been perching, trying to reach for another can, and knocked over Stewart's from the floor beside him. The gold liquid scurried away between the floorboards.

'Ach, ye hun, ye,' said Stewart, 'ye fuckin' mongol, whit are ye?'

'Ach, ah'm sorry, Stewart,' said Joe, on his hands and knees. 'Ah lost ma balance there.' He took the last two cans from the tray and handed one across.

'Okay, okay,' said Stewart, 'ye cannae help bein' a spastic.' He and Joe opened their cans together and drank in silence.

'Whit ah'm sayin' . . .' said Dougie.

'Ah've thought . . .' said Joe.

'Oh Christ,' said Dougie.

'Hoo's about – "*Glasgow* Says No"?'

'Aw well, well,' said Paddy, 'noo ye're talkin'.'

'It's no' bad, that, it's no bad,' said Stewart, inhaling and passing the joint to Joe. 'That's got a wee bit o' style to it, has it no'?'

'Aye, well,' said Alec.

'Aye, well,' said Dougie.

'Naw, it's guid that, it's guid,' said Stewart. 'You're ma man, Joe.' Joe smiled modestly and passed the joint towards Paddy, who was staring up at the sky darkening outside, lost to them all.

'Paddy. Paddy, son,' said Joe, tapping his arm.

'Naw . . . naw . . .' said Paddy, struggling to his feet in the grip of revelation. 'No' Glasgow, no' jest Glasgow – "*Scotland! Scotland* says No!"'

'Oh.' There was one deep exhalation of breath through the whole room as they saw it, simultaneously, clear as a vision, the vast white letters on red, the unequivocal protesting shout. For a while there was nothing to say. They sat, privately smiling, drinking the beer, passing the joint around, sharing the moment.

'We'll need a fuck of a big piece of paper,' said Dougie.

'Naw, naw,' said Alec, 'no' paper. Sheets.'

'Sheets?' said Stewart. 'How d'ye mean? Like bed-sheets, ye mean?'

'Aye, bed-sheets. White bed-sheets. Like . . . fifty of them.'

'Sewn taegether.'

'Aye, sewn taegether.'

'That's brilliant,' said Joe. 'Sheets.'

'Dyed red,' said Paddy.

'Aye.'

'Aye, right.'

'That's brilliant.'

And they sat on, in silence, contemplating the beauty of it, as the light faded, till all the beer was gone.

'Ah'm gettin' cold,' said Joe, finally.

They stumbled to their feet and made their way through the dark hallway to the door.

'When is it she's comin' onyway, Alec?' said Stewart.

'Ach, ah don't know, a few days ah think,' said Alec. He

reached his hand through the splintered hole where the locks had been, and pulled. 'Whit the fuck day is it today onyway?' he said.

It was dark on the landing. They felt their way to the lift, but the lift was out, so they were trailing heavy-footed down the endless stairs at the moment when, outside, through the ruins of the afternoon, the motorcade drove by.

HEROES
Carole Morin

When I was ten she shaved my head. She shaved my head so that I wouldn't catch lice from the boys at school and pass them to her. She always regretted sending me to a mixed school.

But I liked being bald. I stuck my head underwater in the bath, immersing it in foam. That made it flake. Then she decided to let my hair grow in so that she wouldn't have to keep buying razors.

She was very anti-men. But she always had these Big Honeys. One was called Honey Steve. Though the honey was always bracketed. We just called him Steve. When really we were thinking (Honey) Steve. Then there was Honey Sam. Another was Honey Dave, which makes me think of a song. The others I can't remember well because I don't live with her now.

I moved to a building in Bayswater. I'm on the third floor. There's a cupboard right next to my room which the landlord spends a lot of time in. God knows why because I went in there myself once and it smelled. His name's Hosie. He looks like a pineapple but stinks of Paco Rabanne, and has blond hair with dark roots showing. I hear him in that cupboard regularly, usually in the afternoon. The wall that the cupboard shares with my room creaks and if there's someone in my room at the time they look towards the wall and I say: 'It's okay, it's just the landlord.' I would die if anyone thought I lived in a building with rats.

Upstairs there's a Central European who looks like the supporting star of a British B-horror movie. He says hello creatively when we pass on the narrow stairway. On my floor there's a sweaty Irishman with a look about him. He came to my door last Sunday at 7.40 a.m., wearing a baggy flesh-coloured sweatshirt. I could see his nipples through it. He said, 'Good Mornin',' wiped the back of his hand across his nose, coughed defensively, then gave me permission to use the dustbin in the alley.

'Thanks,' I said. 'I never knew there was a bin round there.'

'I'm glad I told you,' he said. Then he didn't say anything. Then he said, 'I'll tell you something else. All the burglars in this building have keys.'

I didn't know what to say. He didn't either. He went back into his room, but didn't lock his door.

The girl next room to me is Korean with bleached hair and red eye make-up. The night I moved in she came to my door.

'Can I borrow your kettle?'

'I don't have a kettle,' I said.

'Just for five mins.' (Hands held in prayer.)

'I'd love to lend you my kettle . . .'

'Oh!' she said.

'But I don't have a kettle.'

'Oh,' she said. I started closing my door. 'Look,' she said, smiling flirtatiously, 'I can bring it right back.'

She often entertains at 5 a.m. That's when she finishes work. Sometimes she comes in with a Chinaman, sometimes an American. They could be honeys. I haven't seen them. But it usually wakes me up.

I am not anti-men. Though I'd rather have a soul-mate than a Big Honey – without question. But then Big Honeys aren't attractive to me. They're not Big Honeys to me.

I know a man who's neither a soul-mate nor a Big Honey. I went to his place once and he immediately switched on a video of himself then turned the sound down and played his own record over and over along with the video. I thought he must just be too lazy to get up and switch it off. But he got up and flipped it over. The whole conversation was demos and restaurants. He owns a restaurant, is trying to

HEROES

open another one. We discussed the merits of compact discs, and whether they put people off their eats. Then he stood up, quite slowly really. I thought: this is it, he's going to lunge now. But there wasn't time.

The phone rang. He didn't pick it up. He reached out to the wall for support, then delicately walked out of the room. He was gone for forty minutes. The phone rang twice while he was away. But I didn't answer it either. I was looking around the house, and found a stack of postcards from his wife, who's said to have given him the bowel trouble while trying to poison him. Dean calls him Sick Bum. Dean's a poet I met in Soho. At the Polo Bar. Which is a greasy spoon though I can't stand that expression.

Dean said he was an actor at first. He confessed later that usually gets people interested. And sometimes they let him off with his bill. If he admits being a poet immediately they just laugh. After I'd known him three days he sent me this letter.

Dear Sophiria,
Do not worry about food. I am not a bit hungry. Last week I did a bit of eating. A loaf, a pound of turkey, a lot of cheese and onion crisps (which I have a passion for this month). Quite frankly if someone offered me a chicken and a cooked beefsteak, now, today, I'd drop it in a bin. I have a bag of oranges I feel obligated to fini. And had a very realistic dream about a whole slice of chocolate cake. The choc. covering was thick and dark, but it was a pale sponge with very red jam inside. I could taste it in the dream. (I think that means I am sex-hungry. – Not a hint. I respect your celibacy.) I think that slice of chocolate cake is like an illustration in a book I had as a kid. Ah, happy days. A poet's lot *etcetera*. I have many new forms, and have almost fini my sonnet – the one about our first meeting. I have not met anyone else new at the Polo since.
      Earnestly,
      Dean

I wrote back.

> Dear Dean,
> I have no kitchen otherwise I would invite you for dinner. Also I cannot cook. My mother always said, 'You'll never get a husband if you can't cook.' But I don't want a husband, I want a soul-mate. (Not a hint.) I read in *Elle* that 'girls with thin lips are not destined to succeed'. Thank God I can pout.
> Yours,
> S.

Dean is impressed by my building. He stood outside it one night he couldn't sleep. He waited until he saw the Korean go in then went home to bed. Sometimes he writes poems during insomnia, but that jaunt to my place had its uses, he told me. He wrote a poem the next day about the merits of living in the heart of a big city without cash.

There are advantages to this area. For example, we have an all-night Bureau de Change. I have never needed currency exchanged in the middle of the night, but I am comforted that the Bureau is there. It is always busy at 3 a.m. That's the latest I stay out. 'A young girl out after three's up to no good.' My mother said that. Most of her maxims are jobbie, but I like that one.

There are other things to see on the walk home. People go along Edgware Road with cabbages and pasta. I have never bought a cabbage in the middle of the night. If I did buy one, I would have nowhere to cook it until next day, when I might borrow someone's kitchen for the event, though by that time the cabbage would have wilted. And I don't enjoy eating vegetables anyway. And grocery shopping is not the sort of activity that appeals to me. Though I admit that, if I was going to indulge in it more often, I would probably do it at night. Occasionally I buy an expensive can of Coke on my way home. I drink it in the morning because being out late gives me a sore throat. 'Be thankful that's all it gives you,' she used to say.

These late nights are part of rather a formal plan to get a

man, though I did meet one outside the bank once during the day. I dropped my cashpoint card. He picked it up. Then he offered me a Mars bar he hadn't had in his mouth yet.

'You can share it if you like,' I said.

'I think I was going to,' he said.

We went to dinner then he kissed me. There were no tongues. But he decided to stick with his regular. She has her own flat in Earl's Court.

I keep up my search, aware that spontaneity is usually the essence of such a discovery. But love's a different experience for us all. Anything goes. He who seeks not finds not. And all those other things my mother – who never had trouble getting Honeys – used to say. And probably still does for all I know. I hope so because I feel more secure when people don't keep changing their philosophies as the notion takes them.

I did meet a man eventually. It was during the day. Dean saw us together in Old Compton and wrote a poem.

'Let's see it,' I said.

'Wait a minute,' he said, fumbling for it in his pocket. 'I just have to check a few points first.' He settled over in his chair then said, 'He's masculine but not over handsome, isn't he?' That could apply so I said, 'Mmhm.'

'He's not so young, is he? But not an old boy?'

I nodded.

'A bit of dark hair,' Dean went on, 'and jeans that have gone a bit loose.'

'What do you mean?'

'As if he just lost weight,' Dean said. Well, he could've lost weight. He's got some to lose, most of us do.

'Just let me see that poem,' I said.

But the poem wasn't about me and Math at all. Dean and I decided he must've been watching the wrong couple. There's a girl going around looks like me.

I knew how much I like Math when I started having fantasies about going bald. In case he ever does. 'I'd like to come home with you sometime,' he said one night. I can't

go home with him because he lives with somebody. But I read in *Elle* it's best to keep an area of your life secret. Or mysterious – maybe that was the word. So I said:
'Let's just do it in this alley.'
'Do what?' he asked.
'Sex,' I said.
I had taken my pants off already. He unloosened his jeans. I always imagine that sort of thing is cold, but it wasn't. I mean draughty on your bum. But I didn't notice the cold. I noticed other things, like his left ear. It has a brownish mark on the edge of the lobe. It looked like a bite or a scab but I could tell it was really wax or dirt. Which is bad enough. I saw other stuff as well. But I suppose it isn't really his fault.

The sex was interesting enough. Followed by the practical bore of what to do with the secretions. We didn't have any paper. And there was the tension of whether people, or dogs, would come and watch. Or if anything was crawling through his jeans which were bunched around his ankles on the ground. Math didn't seem bothered by that at all. He got too into what he was doing. We didn't do it again though. Once is a thrill twice would be a bore, I always say.

Last Sunday I went to see her. She still has her hair. She came to the door in a floral feminine wrap. The sort with make-up stains on the collar and hanging off a bit at the front.

'Hello,' she said, climbing back upstairs, 'if I'd known you were coming . . .' Her voice trailed off because she went into the toilet. Or she may just have finished talking. A man with a not too promising profile stuck his head round the living-room door. 'Are we nearly there Myra?' he called out, staring at me. He had round shoulders and bits of ash in his moustache.

I went up to the toilet and watched my mother. She was hunched over the mirror backcombing her hair. 'I'm no chicken,' she said to herself. Then she lifted her cigarette from where it was balanced on top of the medicine cabinet. She sucked on the cigarette, but continued to shred her hair through the big pink comb. There were hairs in the sink basin, some dark ones. She hadn't flushed the toilet.

'He isn't much of a looker,' I said.

'Frank's a very pleasant man,' she said.

'But not much of a looker.' I could have said more.

'I always say a man's face isn't important, it's the humour underneath it,' she said, scurrying into her bedroom. I paused and then followed. I sat down on the bed, then got up and walked around the room. She was examining herself in another mirror. Come to think of it my mother isn't a looker herself. She belongs to that class of women who consider it unfeminine to remove unfortunate hair. I had never been curious before to know how a woman like her could attract so many Honeys. Honeys are said to be particular. I said, 'Have you got some money someplace?'

'Of course not dear,' she was throwing things in her bag. 'What an idea,' she cackled. 'I'm always in it for love.' Then she made a nervous noise and ran to the top of the stairs. 'Just a mo Frank,' she called downstairs, then ran back into the room. 'I think about him last thing, then when I wake in the morning I think about him again.' She said this without a trace of embarrassment. Then she pulled off her robe. Underneath there was this tight nylon-looking sweater women with sagging breasts shouldn't go near. It was orange, and the neck was all rolled back. She pulled the neck up, still looking in the mirror.

The last thing I think about each night is my teeth. I would hate to be toothless. Lying in bed, I actually have to remember cleaning them. And still be able to taste the paste. Otherwise I must get up and do them again. I have to. Or I can't sleep. Then when I wake up in the morning I can't do a thing until I've scrubbed them again. I am not one of those girls who can roll over, stretch, and grab a doughnut from the bedside table. I can't even put a tape on without dealing with the plaque build-up first. It collects on them in the night. No matter how clean you are. A dentist I kissed once told me that.

She grabbed her bag and lit another cigarette. 'Good seeing you,' she said.

'He's a creep,' I said.

'Same to you,' she said.

She went to the top of the stairs then walked back. She looked at me with her serious face. 'You'll often find in your life dear that the big handsome Honey of a man prefers the more modest woman.' I looked at her. 'It sets him off better,' she added.

'What's that supposed to mean?'

'Oh you,' she said. 'We must go – come and see us again though.'

I used her phone to call Dean. Then I met him in the Polo. I went into the toilet when I arrived and repainted my lips. I love my lips. As I was shading them I came to a decision. I decided to try that alley again with Math. To let him kiss or lick all this paint off. Men are said to enjoy that – who knows? Whichever he prefers. For he isn't really the soulful type. More sexy. Dean's the soulful one even though, being a poet, it's embarrassing for him to be soulful. And I'm not even sure it's a soul-mate I'm interested in now anyway.

THE MIRACLE OF JONAH
William Raeper

an now the ground wiz steamin, the pavements still brownwet frae the rain, aye, it was ane doolie sessoun richt enough that Spring Equinox. But whaur were the thochts o Danny Patterson as he stood in the bluescraped bus shelter wi the wire glass a smashed that Sunday. Aye, that Sunday when the buses are ower late an hardly seem to come at a.

Eleanor, takin the washin in, snatchin shirts an socks an underwear aff the line an talkin ower the fence to Heather Fraser. 'Unner my feet,' she had said. 'He's aye unner my feet.' He had heard her. Then the rain rappit the earth, like arrowis sore, like it wiz a hedgehog earth, all sore wi the rappit rain. When it stopped, Danny had gone to get a bus down to the High Street. He's aye unner my feet was still in his aye in my hair aye unner my skin. Aye, in a year of marriage, he had got quite far.

'Whaur are ye goin?' Eleanor let a handfu o clothes pegs roll on the kitchen table.

'Oot.'

Danny put down the *Sunday Mail*, put on his coat, an went.

The sone was michtily obscurit of his licht that day, but when the clouds cracked, that sent the ground steamin. Danny waited for a bus, there, in the shelter, wi a couple o kids. The buses aye took a long time on a Sunday, that slack, long day o rest, that day when nothing seems to come, when little seems to happen.

It had been Sattirday, aye, anither, different kin' o day, the day before. It had been the day o Henderson's dance. For it wid be Easter soon an they aye laid on a dance. Eleanor had come back wi a dress frae Markies an laid it oot on the bed. Then she had phoned her mither to tell her what she had bocht. 'It's braw – aye – but it wisna cheap. But ye ken, wi Markies, it'll last. It's worth the money. Aye – that's richt. The nicht – the dance is the nicht. Oh, Danny's got his suit.'

Danny's suit had hung on the wardrobe rail frae way back last year's end to this. He had been married in it and had not worn it since. He had never liked wearin a suit an now it reminded him o that day. His weddin.

Grit aboundance and blind prosperitie oftymes makis ane evill conclusion. Danny squeaked open the shiny wooden door. The wardrobe, like most of the other furniture, had come from Eleanor's parents.

'Aye,' said Eleanor comin up in her underskirt. 'Ye'll look braw in that. But mind an polish yer shoes now. Ye know what ye're like.'

'Aye – we'll . . .'

'Six o'clock! I'll have to have a bath.' She took off her watch. 'The taxi's comin at half-past seven.'

'The taxi? Can we no tak the bus?'

Eleanor laughed, clearin her throat. 'That wid jist be like you, wouldn't it? The bus! You wid really tak the bus.' She shook her head. 'Sometimes,' she said, 'I wonder what I've married.'

The wedding picture wiz on the sideboard downstairs. Eleanor wiz in lacy white; Danny wiz in his suit, stiff, because it wiz now tight around his waist – though he did not want to admit it. The picture wiz there, on the sideboard, taken on the steps of Highfield parish church. Danny and

Eleanor were both smiling. You couldn't deny it now. It wiz in the photograph.

Slane with schouris were the flowers o the Spring Equinox, there, that Sunday, when the bus finally arrived. It wiz a number twelve, red and double-decker, advertisin whisky on its side. The bus coughed, its brakes hissin, to a stop. Danny got on and climbed up the narrow metal stairs to the top deck. NO SPITTING it said. No, but you could smoke. Danny took out a packet o cigarettes.

'What are ye – oh, not now! I've got to change.' Danny put his hand on Eleanor's thigh. She brushed it away like a dead fly. Her colour rose. She was sittin wi a hairbrush in her hand.
  'Oh, come on,' he said, lyin down beside her in his underwear on the bed, the bed her parents had given them. He stroked her leg wi his forefinger.
  'If I let you have yer ain way, I'd never be aff my back. As it is,' she picked up a pair o tights, 'I'm never aff my feet.'
  'Oh, come on.' Danny was like ane licherus bull. As with the glaikis he wer ouirgane. How could she say no? They were married – he – prised open her legs – he – pushed her back on to the bed – and – oh – and – oh – hir hips gaff mony hiddous cry – he was – oh – sic – a – sic – a – fool.
  How mony men in operation ar like to beistis in conditioun.
  Eleanor was panting. She stopped. She sat up. 'I'll have to wash again,' she said. 'I hope we're no going to be late. Are ye satisfied now?'

The day wox dirk, sae dirk it wox. The bus passed Highfield Kirk whaur they had got married. There was an iron gate and a gravel drive up to the big, big door. Outside stood a signboard wi a poster pasted onto it, curly and unstuck at the edges: An evil and adulterous generation seeketh after a sign; and there shall no sign be given to it, but the sign of the prophet Jonas . . .

Danny had not moved far since he had got married to Eleanor. He had always taken the number twelve to the High Street, even from a boy. He had always sat on the upper-deck, except when he went into town wi Eleanor who did not like the smoke. So now, on the top deck, he wiz many Dannys, all Dannys, all there had ever been, crowded thegither on the journey – the journey past the miracle of Jonah – Jonah who had lain three days in the belly o the big fish. Danny remembered that story from somewhere; maybe from bible at school maybe. He wondered whaur he could get anither packet o cigarettes. He pit the last one into his mouth.

Now the Lord had prepared a great fish to swallow up Jonah. And Jonah was in the belly of the fish three days and three nights.

'Are ye ready?' Eleanor was. She had put on her nail varnish. Carefully. She had had her hair done. Earlier. Now she wiz in her new Markies dress.

'Well?' She stood in front o Danny.

'Well what?' Danny wiz lacin up his shoes.

'Do I look nice?'

'Yes, you look fine.'

'Fine. Is that all ye can say? Fine!'

There wiz a parp and the hum o a runnin motor frae downstairs. Eleanor parted the bedroom curtains.

'Taxi's here. Right. Have ye got money?'

'Aye.'

'Fine.'

Ye brak my hart, my bony ane.

> To part fra Phebus did Aurora grete
> Hir cristall teris I saw hyng on the flouris
> Quhilk he for lufe all drank up with his hete.

At the Shell garage, the bus went down Hendry Road, past harled houses under rusty eaves and squares o tended gardens, then up, up the hill to Forth Park and the Foreign Legion. There was a doctor who lived in a house called Kilmeny and there, from the top o the hill, just by the cemetery wall, you could see the Forth, spread incandescent and clear, all the way ower to Lothian, Berwick and the Bass Rock. Here the bus coughed, hissed and shuddered, gainin as it hurled down the hill, down to the railway line, past whaur the linoleum factories had been, down, down, to whaur Danny could see the roll o the kettle-drum hills and the twin concrete stumps o Seafield Pit.

'It's the Sinclair Hotel, is it?' said the taxi driver. He had a cassette on in his car. 'I hear the sound of distant drums' filled the back whaur Eleanor an Danny got in.
  'Yes,' said Eleanor.
  'Right-o, an ye want me to pick ye up?'
  'Near twelve,' said Eleanor.
  'Right-o.'
  Danny sat, his trousers circling his waist, like the Forth circled Fife, like

> fowllis in forrest that sang cleir
> Now walkis with a drery cheir.

That Spring Equinox Sunday, when the steam wiz comin aff the streets.

'There's a buffet, isn't there?' said Eleanor, takin aff her coat. 'Well, tak aff yer coat, then!'
  'Hello Danny. Hello Eleanor.'
  'Hello Dougie. Hello Jean.'
  The bar wiz lit an lined wi uncomfortable-lookin men. Men tryin to shed their wives on this o all uncomfortable nights. The men dangled on the bar stools, catchin each other wi talk, cigarette smoke windin in a grey string

frae their fingers, wi whisky doused in watter at their hands, wi the dark dark pints o heavy at their elbows. They were here, they, on this, the most uncomfortable o all nights.

An the next dance will be a quickstep.

There was a band in the corner – fower middlin men in satin red shirts. One on keyboards, one accordion, one drums, one guitar. They were called The Forth Band.

And now a country an western number.

'Do ye want to dance?' said Danny.

'Let's have a seat first,' said Eleanor, looking round. 'Are Colin an Jackie here?' There wiz a wave.

'Ower there,' said Danny.

'So they are.' Eleanor led Danny through the few couples already on the dance floor to a table near the corner o the room. It wiz a little too near the band for Eleanor's likin.

'Fine do,' said Colin, noddin wi approval at the bar, the band an the dancers.

'Are ye goin to get me a drink?' said Eleanor.

'Sure,' said Danny, 'whit wid ye like?'

Eleanor hummed, throwin back her heid. 'Vodka an orange,' she said. 'It's a special occasion.' Then she laughed. An Jackie laughed too.

Danny pushed his way to the front o the bar. Ted McKenzie wiz beside him. He wiz rubbin a fiver atween his fingers.

'I have to bring the wife to this every year,' he said. 'An it's always the same. Dances are too much for the likes o me. I like my ain fireside. But my wife – she has a whale o a time.'

'Aye,' said Danny, handin the barman a couple o green notes an some change. The vodka had arrived, an a pint o heavy.

> Yisterday fair up sprang the flouris
> This day thai ar all slane with schouris.

When the bus reaches the railway bridge, it turns right and goes along past the station. The museum, granite and classical, is there too, an the War Memorial Gardens. The Adam Smith Halls are on the left-hand side. There's a roundabout, an Rollo's garage. The bus crosses the roundabout and drives past the Post Office and the Town Hall wi its narrow, singular clock. There, finally is the bus station. There, finally is whaur the bus stops.

When Danny got back to his table wi the drinks, there wiz somebody else there.

'I think,' said Eleanor drily, 'that you two already know each ither.'

It was Lorraine Mitchell, wi a tan.

'What are ye doin here?' said Danny. Surprise choked his voice.

'Back for a holiday,' laughed Lorraine. She lit a cigarette and blew the smoke out in a widenin spray above her head.

'Whaur've ye been?'

'Oh, this?' She looked at her bare arms. She feigned surprise. 'The Canary Islands. The only place at this time o year wi guaranteed sunshine. It wiz braw.'

'What's it like in . . .'

'. . . oh, fine, fine!' said Lorraine quickly, smiling. 'Just fine. I'm hame to see my mither.'

Lorraine was brown wi bleached hair an a dress cut low in front o her. She looked good. She had always looked good. Always.

'What about a dance then?' asked Lorraine, stubbing out her cigarette in the cutglass ashtray.

'Oh, aye.'

Danny took Lorraine by the hand and led her out into the floor. He had taken dancing lessons at the school and knew how to dance. That always made him popular at dos like this whaur the husbands were often unwilling or unable to come out for anythin except the 'Hokey-cokey' an 'Auld Lang Syne'.

Should auld acquaintance be forgot and never brought to mind.

'I didn't think I'd see you here,' blared Lorraine through the music, close to Danny's ear. Danny wiz holdin her close. Eleanor wiz watchin.

'Why's that?' Danny smiled at her and warmed a little. He screwed up his mouth.

'I always thought ye'd leave – here, I mean.'

'Oh, Eleanor likes it here.'

'And you, what about you, do you like it here?' Danny shrugged. 'It's fine by me,' he said.

Lorraine shook her head. It wiz hard to hear. 'As long as ye're happy,' she said.

'Oh, happy, I don't think about that!'

Lorraine was slim and light. She was very yielding. She had been yielding before. Then she had gone away.

'You only get yer chances once, you know,' said Lorraine.

'Now you sound like my mither,' laughed Danny. He brought Lorraine back to the table an let his arm rest on hers, just that little bit too long, lettin himsel feel the warmth o her through her dress. *Cacis perillous.* Eleanor span an span the ice cubes round in her glass o vodka.

'She's away frae her husband. That bleached hair. I don't know what ye saw in her. Wagglin hersel at everybody.'

'I didna see anythin in her.' I nevir wowit weycht bot yow.

Eleanor an Danny were in the taxi back.

'Don't you lie to me – it was obvious. Colin an Jackie were really embarrassed fur me. No one knew whaur tae look – except you!' Eleanor fingered her neck. Her face wiz chalk an set. 'All I wanted – all I wanted – wiz fur things tae look braw, for us to hae a good time – an – then you have to go an . . .'

'Here, here.'

'Don't you touch me.' For verray pietie scho began to greit. But Danny did not withdraw his hand and sat strokin the tips o Eleanor's fingers in her lap. She did no protest, but she did no encourage.

THE MIRACLE OF JONAH

Ane doolie sessoun, at the Spring Equinox, when the streets were brown an steamin after a shower o rain, Jonah prayed unto the Lord his God out of the fish's belly.

Danny walked out o the bus station, across the High Street and down, ower the prom, to the beach. There had been sand here once, now washed grey by shale frae the pit. The hump o Berwick Law wiz clear, pencilled in the distance. There were bones there, o a whale. Danny had seen them once when he wiz a boy. He had had the chance o a school trip.

'You only get yer chances once, you know.'

Danny was angry. He kicked a tin can. He threw a flat stone into the mild, languid waves. They hissed into foam on the flat, seaweedy sand. There was a salt smell of dank sewerage from the sea. Danny turned up his nose.

'Aye unner my feet aye in my hair aye unner my skin.'

The mone sould thoill ecclipis.

It would be Easter soon, Easter. All Danny could do now wiz tae get the bus back home.

It would be Easter soon, Easter.

Danny took a last look at the sea. He wisna sure if he could be braw again.

THE SIGHTING
Moira Burgess

I'd hardly got the gas lit and my corsets off when Archie Graham came up the stair. God, I thought, that's a surprise! Gave him my usual patter, of course, just as if I'd never seen him before in my life; but wondering all the time, has holy Mary put the bar up altogether? By the very look of her, the hat with a veil and the gloves and the hymn book, you can tell she only allows it every second Sunday between the hours of three and four, and not then if the minister's just reminded her that to be carnally minded is death.

He couldn't do a thing. I wasn't surprised; trouble takes some people that way, and he's had his troubles since Christmas. To see him dottering between the chair and the bed you'd have said he was just home from the front, shell-shocked or all gassed to rags. God knows I've had plenty of them to deal with, so I treated him the same way. Kind of gentle. No use.

'Never heed,' I finally said. 'Never bother your arse, son. Sit for a minute, eh?' I don't very often let them do that; well, time's money. Only I kept thinking about his wife Mary laughing in the street.

And he was thinking about that night too. 'A' those Christmas presents,' he kept saying. 'An' a wee dress an' coat. I telt her she should wait till we got word, but it was six weeks, ken? They usually let them out after six weeks.'

I said 'Aye, sure,' still soothing; though it gave me a stound, remembering the wee dress and coat. Just the same age, three and a bit. I thought that right away, couldn't help it, when I saw Mary Graham holding them up to show her friend Mrs Bain.

'Six weeks,' she was saying in her little mim voice. 'She'll get home any time now. Maybe today. They discharge them on a Tuesday.' And there she stood with her bag full of books and toys. Their lot doesn't make anything of Christmas as a rule; I remember thinking she'd get a black mark from the minister. 'Archie went to see her yesterday,' she was saying. 'You're allowed to see them through glass, you know? Well, he didn't actually see her, they didn't want to disturb her, she was playing with a new dolly, they said. But she'll be home soon. This is Tuesday, isn't it?' And she laughed so hearty; she was out of herself, you'd say. She didn't even notice me squeezing past the two of them to get into the baker's. Well, I've got to eat like anybody else, haven't I? You wouldn't think I should, from some of the looks they turn on me.

I had to squeeze past again when I came out; she was still gossiping there, so happy that she didn't even draw her skirts aside. Thinking about that, I nearly bumped into Father Connolly. 'Hullo, Father,' I said, just as I always do. Why shouldn't I, after all? Mind you, it's many a strange answer I get.

But he was looking past me. 'Isn't that Mrs Graham laughing there?'

'That's right.' I think he knew all along. He was shaking his head; he's a young chap, he looked ready to burst out crying. 'She can't know. She can't know. Perhaps I should tell her,' he was saying. 'But it would come better from one of her own.'

She'd moved off down the street at last. 'If you want to catch her, Father, now's your chance,' I told him, since he was dithering on. 'Yon's her house at the corner, where . . .'

'Where the two nurses are standing,' he said.

And we watched as Mary Graham reached her house. As she saw the nurses. As they spoke to her and led her along the street. One of them carried the bag of Christmas presents, with a bit of broderie anglaise sticking out at the top. Maybe the sash of the wee dress.

'I was at the hospital,' Father Connolly said. I think he'd

forgotten I was there. 'I asked who the wee girl was, so ill in the side ward. "Tibbie Graham – she'll not live," they said.'

Archie was still going on. 'I've been doing what I shouldna since. Drinking, ken?' He began to laugh that uncanny way; it's not safe to stop them, though I could hear shuffling on the landing where the next client had arrived. 'I went into town, I bought a horse and gig, sixty-five pound it cost. We canna afford it. We dinna even need it.' He gripped his hands between his knees. 'But it's her. She'll no' cry. She's never cried.'

'Right enough,' I said, 'that's no' natural.' Though I was thinking: she's likely no' very good at crying. She's never had anything to cry about in her life before. Mary Graham? She's aye been a lucky bitch.

The next client seemed to be losing patience; he was kicking the banisters as a hint. 'Well,' I said, 'that's your time up, son.'

But then he said, 'And it's Tuesday again. Tuesdays is the worst.'

'Tuesday, Wednesday,' I said, 'what's the odds?' I wasn't very civil, for the customer outside, having given up, was stamping down the stairs.

'She goes down to the hospital every Tuesday,' he said, 'to watch for the wean coming out. She's down there now.'

For a minute I was stumped for what to say. I remembered the wee white coffin, the heavy slow horses in the street where all the blinds were down. Mary's pal Mrs Bain didn't leave her house for a week. I hadn't a customer for two days; a thing like that, I've noticed, sends them back to their wives. But they wouldn't have got very good value from me.

At last I said, 'But didn't you – didn't she – see the wean? They usually – let you see.' As he looked at me, I added 'So I've heard.' None of his business how I knew. Not after all those years.

'Aye, we saw her,' he said, 'lying there. But the wee lassie we saw, she had dark hair, short and dark. Our Tibbie had fair hair, all curls.'

'Scarlet fever does that,' I said.

It was hard to take, the way he went on. 'Does it? You're sure? You've kent it happen?'

'I've kent it,' was the best I could find to say.

He knew fine himself. 'Aye, they told her that. Oh, they told her plenty afterwards. Diphtheria, they said, and the stuff they sent for didn't work. Or else it never arrived. We got different stories, ken?' Now he'd started he couldn't be stopped; with one bit of my mind I was wondering if I'd ever get any other customers again. 'But Mary, she thinks – well – there was maybe a mistake. That Tibbie's no' dead at all. And Tuesday's the day they get discharged.'

He was getting up to go at long last. He hovered by the table: 'I'm sorry I couldna . . .'

'It's a' one to me, son,' I said.

'You'll be wantin' . . .'

'Aye, sure,' I said, stowing the money away as usual. Well, you've got to, eh?

Right enough, I didn't get any other customers all night. I reckoned that bad-tempered bugger that stamped downstairs had put the word around that I was away, or worse. I sat there and smoked and thought about scarlet fever. And wee lassies. And other thoughts I needn't mention. I kept coming back to holy Mary Graham, with her veil and her hymn book, and the skirt that swished aside when I passed, but swished nowhere else her Bible didn't allow. Late on, seeing the night was a wash-out anyway, I put on my hat – and it cost twice what Mary Graham's did, I'll tell you – and went down to the hospital.

To let you understand, there's a kind of porch there, with glass doors between it and the main corridor, along which wee lassies come when they've got over the scarlet fever; or don't come, as the case may be. The doors were locked now, and the lights in the corridor turned low, but Mary Graham was still in the porch, I suppose she'd been there all night; maybe the nurses hadn't noticed her, or maybe they'd given up telling her to go away. She was sitting slumped on a bench in a corner, with her respectable skirts all rucked up

THE SIGHTING

and her hat over her eyes. Sad and mad and exhausted, she'd fallen asleep.

I'd come to laugh at her. At least I think I had. You ken a' about it now, Mary, I'd have said, supposing she'd been awake to hear. A lot of good it's done you, eh, the Bible and the husband and the skirts that pull aside? You ken now how it feels, Mary, was what I meant to say.

Only it got twisted round in my mind. I'd had a hell of a day: a client who couldn't do the business, and losing me all those others who could. It all got back to front some way: the words, or what they meant. Although she's so bloody good, I found myself saying, she feels the same now as I did then.

I took a step forward, and Mary Graham jumped awake.

She was looking straight at me. Was she? Her eyes switched back and forth; they looked at me, but then they moved to look at something beside me. It was icy cold in the porch; I'd never felt the like. I didn't dare to turn my head. There wasn't anything beside me. Was there, though?

'Mary! Are you there, Mary?' shouted Archie Graham outside.

She kind of gasped and turned. As he came in, sobs burst out of her, jumbled up with words. 'Tibbie's dead, Archie, she's dead.' She sounded nearly happy; why should that be? 'She was in her nightgown, the last one I made her. I saw her. And beside her – beside her . . .'

She stuck there as if there was something worse to come. He patted her and muttered till she got it out. I'd pulled myself back into the darkest corner; he never saw me yet.

'That woman in the town, Archie, that terrible woman. No, you don't know, how should you? She's got a house – where she – no, I can't say it . . .'

His patting and muttering speeded up a bit, but she was going on.

'I know now, Archie. Tibbie dying, it was maybe all for the best. I had a . . .' Her tongue was slow with tears; she stumbled for words, and came up with a strange one. 'I had a sighting of that woman to tell me so.'

'A what?' Archie said.

'God sent her.' He's hard up for messengers, I thought in my corner as Mary Graham raved on. 'We're not to grieve that Tibbie's dead. God's told me. We don't know what – what she might have been like if she'd grown up.'

She was blubbering enough to flood the porch; did her good, I suppose. I didn't give that much thought as I stood there seeing red. You stuck-up wee cow! I wanted to rage. The bloody cheek of you! Your lassie's better dead, eh, than living like me? You've got your house and your man, and you'll have other weans! It's well and well enough for you!

I didn't say any of that. Her tears began to dry up and she said to Archie, 'I believe I'll maybe sleep tonight.' He put his arm round her and led her away. I dare say she did sleep; or something as good. Anyway I've never had Archie Graham up my stair again. Twice in a lifetime; well, that's not bad. Not that he remembers the first time, or knows how I saw his likeness when the midwife gave me the wean.

I'm vexed at myself, though, that I didn't say any of those things. What held me back? Maybe it was that odd word she came upon. She had a sighting. Not of me – suffering God, I was there, wasn't I? But of a wee lassie in a nightgown.

Not the hospital gown they put on them, far too big and wide. Her own nightgown that she'd wear at home. Round arms coming out of the sleeves, not the sticks the fever melts them to. The right kind of sleepy flush on the wee face, and the curly hair. Something like that it would be, the sighting she had.

Oh, Mary Graham, you lucky bitch.

THE WALL
Justine Cable

'Oh, no! Here we go again,' staff nurse Lippet said.
'What?'
'See that one over there? Lila Parker? That's the second one this week, and the eighth this month.'
Maryanne was baffled. 'What exactly do you mean, staff?'
'You see how she's heading for that empty wall? In here, that means only one thing. She'll be dead inside of three days.'
'Surely that's just a superstition? There can't be anything to that old saying, can there?'
'You'd better believe it, girl. It happens. If you don't believe me, just watch. But in the meantime, she'll make enough work to keep three of you busy.'

Lila had to run an obstacle course to get there. First, Mr Wilson with his motorized wheelchair nearly ran her down. Crazy Vera hopscotched around her with an imaginary stone. Then there were the three monkeys, as everyone called them. Miss Collins was blinded by cataracts, Mrs Baker deaf, and Mr Murray mute from the removal of a cancerous larynx. They propped their feet up on stools so close to the television that there wasn't room for Lila's walker.

There was no choice but to go the long way round the lounge. Coming or going was difficult for everyone, and they had to sidle by in the narrow aisle to avoid entangling each other.

Lila finally reached her goal. The wall was blank, though

against it, a tan leather couch blocked off the lower part. There was a convenient leather seat facing the couch, giving a commanding view of the pastel blue surface. It was perfect.

With difficulty since none of the staff would assist her, Lila lowered herself to the seat, then pushed her walking frame aside. She relaxed her old bones, settling them as comfortably as their nearly fleshless state would allow. Following tradition, she closed her eyes to concentrate her thoughts, then slowly let her lids come open.

With a sharp intake of breath, she saw her dream had come true. Before her, as though through a window, she saw her favourite place. The view of the pasture was from the living room of her house within the shelter of sixty-foot tamaracks. It must be spring: deciduous needles were just beginning to fill the branches.

Off to the right, through trees cleared of undergrowth, she could see the guest house. They were building it with thinned trees from the small woods. She and Joe would take it up to two feet this year, four the next. Their sons used it as an enclosed play area when she and Joe were busy with the land.

Between the house and pasture, they'd dug a firepit for barbecues. A weathered shed protected the summer cookstove from the elements. You really needed two stoves for cooking with wood. The winter one helped warm the house, but in summer its heat drove you outside. The alternative was salads all summer, and neither Joe nor the boys would tolerate that for long.

But in the pasture she saw what warmed her heart most about this place, aside from her family. In the pasture was her beloved grey mare, Joe's roan Appaloosa brood mare, and the nine-week-old foal, his white blanket having the minimum five spots needed to register him. They'd just brought in a stallion to service his dam, and the silly fool thought he could challenge a full-grown horse for possession of the two mares. Lila ran out, not knowing how to separate them. Luckily, the newcomer was gentle of temperament, and put the foal in his place with a nip. How she loved to watch them run for the sheer joy of it!

She turned to the pigs, Dotty and Albert, just off to the left of the clearing. They happily wallowed in dust in the drought, and kept their drinking trough immaculate. At feeding time, they'd climb the rails, grunting for a scratch behind the ears before diving into the mixed rations.

Maryanne interrupted her reverie, shaking her to attention. 'It's lunch time, Mrs Parker.' She smiled and took hold of the reedy arm. 'Let's get you up and started for the dining room.'

Without any warning, Lila started pained, shrill screaming. 'No! No!' she shrieked.

'What's all this, now?' staff asked, hurrying through the turtle crush of the elderly bound for the bright spot of the day – meal time.

'I don't know what's wrong. I just tried to help her up for lunch. Did I do it wrong? I didn't *hurt* her, did I?'

'No, you didn't. They just get like this when the time comes.'

'You mean, what you said was *true*?'

During the discussion, Lila went back to looking at the wall. As long as she could see it, she felt comfortable. But if someone made her lose her concentration, she felt an almost physical wrenching at her heart. The two younger women got on either side of her and began to lift. Staff got in front of her picture and Lila screamed again.

'She just won't go. Not without a hell of a fuss, and she'll get some of the others started.' Staff was disgusted at capitulating. 'There's nothing for it. Bring a tray in for her. And if she won't feed herself, you'll have to do that, too.'

Maryanne didn't mind feeding Lila. If she covered any part of the wall from view, Lila would start the racket, so she was careful not to lift the fork too high. She felt satisfied when she looked down at the empty plate. Mrs Parker was a picky eater, but she hadn't noticed that she was eating.

What she was not prepared for was the smell that started five minutes later. Maryanne turned a bright shade of red, embarrassed for the patient. Mrs Parker had no history of incontinence.

Staff looked grim. 'I told you she'd be trouble. Now we have to change her. And there'll be that godawful noise. Come on.'

They got a grip on the avidly staring Lila's arms. Encircling her waist, they frogmarched her to her bed. Pulling the curtains, they undressed her gently, despite her incessant chalk-on-blackboard screeching. They put her into a hospital gown and diapers – street clothes would be pointless when she'd just do it again.

'Can we put her back by the wall?' Maryanne suggested. 'Maybe she'll stop this screaming.'

'Oh, it'll stop, all right. But it won't change anything. Still, it would be quieter in here. She's getting Miss Collins started. *She* takes several minutes to get into full cry, but then only meal time can stop her.' Puzzled at Lila's need, they returned Lila to her wall, leaving her to stare at it.

It was winter now, the combination of drifts and ploughing left an eight foot embankment. Just across the pasture was a lovely Scotch pine. She laughed out loud as Joe chopped the tree four feet from the ground, the right size for Christmas. That year, they'd made all their presents. Even young Robbie had found bits of ropes, string and yarn to wind into a ball for all of them to toss.

When the pine started to grow again, they were delighted. The three topmost branches curved upward, looking for all the world like a Turkish dome. Years later, two of them would be used for the runners of a rocking chair. But that was still to be.

She was so engrossed in the image that she didn't hear Mr Wilson's wheelchair approach. She was concentrating on the tree when suddenly it changed.

'That's a silly looking tree,' he growled. The tree

straightened, lost two of the surrogate trunks, and stood ramrod straight. 'If you're going to do this at all, why don't you bother to get things right?'

Lila tore her eyes from the wall. 'You leave me alone! That's the way the tree *was*!' Her screech was loud enough to wake Mrs Baker.

'You don't have to shout! I'm just trying to show you how to make it better!'

'But I don't want it so-called better. The way it was is just fine. Better than better!'

'And what happens when it's finished?' he demanded. 'Then you feel like you can finally curl up and die. Just like the others.'

'That's my right, isn't it? And no business of yours!'

Mr Wilson sat looking at the wall. A black gelding appeared in the pasture.

'Get that thing out of there! There's not enough grass for him.'

'But there is, woman! There is if I put it there. And I will. Next time.' And with that, he wheeled himself away.

Lila stopped moaning and contemplated the horse. He *did* look good there. Maybe she could leave him for a while, if Mr Wilson would feed him.

Two weeks later, Lila Parker was still alive, in control of her plumbing, but steadfastly avoiding communal meals. She refused to leave the wall, except at night. It was all right then, because there was always night after day, and nobody had to watch everything all the time.

Mr Wilson popped by occasionally, his arthritic hands working the buttons of his wheelchair. True to his word, he'd fed the black. 'All you've got there is alfalfa,' he accused. 'That burns too hot for a horse. It's okay for cows, they eat it twice, so to speak. But a horse only has one stomach.' He added timothy grass to the hayfield, interspersing it with the alfalfa. The field was now lush by comparison.

He was in the habit of making little changes in her world, but did nothing that encroached on her memories or what she was doing, so she didn't mind. Sometimes she thought them an improvement, other times she was indifferent. But today, he surprised her.

'That your boundary line up there?'

'No, it's on the other side of the road. We have a little piece all the way to that post.'

'Who lives there?'

Lila thought that a strange question, but answered anyway. 'The Malgars. The only good one of the bunch is the young son, and he'll leave as soon as he's old enough. The others are drunken layabouts.'

'Do you want to get rid of them?'

Lila thought about it a moment. 'I'd have loved it then, but I'm not so sure about now. After all, we went through a lot because of them, and it would be like wiping out part of my life.'

'How about on the other side of them?'

'Nobody ever lived there. It was forestry land. Why?'

Mr Wilson shifted the scene to her boundary and saw the far fence of the Malgars. After that, blurred greenery left the landscape undefined. 'I was thinking I might build up there. You've had the wall for a long time, and both my arthritis and my diabetes are getting worse. But I don't want to push you out.'

That was the first reference he'd made to the purpose of the wall. It took Lila aback, somehow seeming to desecrate the new meaning she found there. She was about to refuse when he answered her thought.

'Don't worry. It's not like that. It's just that when I come here, I feel better for a while. So I thought if I had a place of my own . . .'

'It *would* be nice to have a neighbour, eh, Mr Wilson,' she smiled shyly. 'But you know, I don't know anything about you, except for your illnesses.'

'That's the way they like it here, isn't it?' he sneered. Then, without a word, he began erecting a building. He

didn't put it up all at once, as hers had sprung up, but built from the foundations up, just as he had done during the Depression. The final touch was the sign –
Jas. Wilson & Sons, Greengrocer.

They sat in agreeable silence for a while, seeing the difference the new addition made. Slowly, hesitantly, they began to get to know each other.

The others thought Vera was gaga, but she didn't mind. She knew exactly what she was about. After all, hardly anyone comes to visit spinsters. Her nephew, Phillip, and his wife Shirley had forced her to come here when she forgot to turn off the gas ring, even though no damage was done. She'd be willing to bet that they'd done the same thing at least once.

But here she was. They refused to have her live with them, saying that Shirley couldn't cope with the twin toddlers and another on the way. The alternative was committal, so she'd thought to retain some control by going 'willingly'. Now she was expected to sit here and vegetate, just like the rest.

Oh, she'd tried to get them interested in things like bowling or bridge, but they weren't up to that. So if she wanted some fun, she'd make it herself. She'd quote nursery rhymes when the mood struck her, or let her whole body remember dancing the night away with one of her suitors, humming old tunes when the words escaped her.

She could still play games, even if the others didn't want to. Once, she managed to grab a box of salt from the kitchen when cook wasn't looking. Normally, the nurses salted food for those who were allowed it. It never mattered how much or how little one wanted, one had no control. So Vera took control and graciously offered some to her table mates. They looked at her suspiciously and shook their heads. When they weren't looking, she salted their food. They seemed delighted, but never acknowledged the gift. So she got even, surreptitiously adding salt to the sweetened tea or puddings, then watching their expressions. Disappointingly, only a few noticed a difference.

Her undoing was the visit from Phillip and Shirley. Five weeks late, they finally arrived with something for her to sign – a power of attorney. Supposedly it would authorize them to use some of her money, not all of course, to pay for her 'treatment' here. That was a laugh. They wanted Papa's house. She refused. They countered with an invitation to live with them – wouldn't she like taking care of the twins? She was adamant. They threatened committal, and since she was already under care . . .

She had signed, in the end, the fight gone out of her. Things that gave her pleasure since she'd arrived no longer worked. There was nothing left for it but to square her shoulders and dance her way to the wall. At first, Vera just watched the others, seeing what they were doing, trying to pick out any rules. When she thought she was ready, she asked them if she could join in. They seemed happy enough to have her.

'But I don't want Papa's house,' she was firm. 'I've always wanted a little cottage. Can I do that instead?'

The others discussed it, and asked her a few questions. Yes, she knew just what it was like. After all, she lived there in her dreams. And there was another thing she wanted to change. When she was twenty, she turned down Charlie's proposal. He'd never married, and was killed in the war. Could she rectify her mistake?

That seemed to rock the others. They'd brought their loved ones with them, but governed by the past, they lived out relationships as they had been. This was quite different.

It took a long time to decide the question. Lila held out for replay of reality, but Mr Wilson pointed out that the black horse in her pasture had let in something new. Besides, with all the sorrows in his own life, he would be more than happy to change things. Why should he be forced to relive all the bad things, just to get the good? Mrs Baker agreed. She didn't want to relive her youth, just to regain her hearing. Surely they could improve on the past. After all, whose lives were so perfect that they must be cast in amber? They finally agreed to accept Vera's changes.

'That's the fifth,' staff said to the night sister. 'All day, all they do is sit. Staring. At the wall. It's enough to drive me batty.'

'You're just not hard enough on them,' the older nurse with the bowl haircut told her. 'I don't take any nonsense from them. Ten o'clock, they get their pills, and bed by ten thirty. And that's mostly because we have to undress some.'

'But don't they give you any trouble, getting them away from the wall?' Staff had resigned herself to letting at least one of them eat at the wall, or all five would begin to howl.

'I wouldn't let them,' said the sister whom the patients referred to as 'Little Hitler'. 'What they really want is a strict schedule, with plenty of sleep. Old folks need their sleep. Those five you're talking about? They're probably just dozing.'

'I wouldn't bet on it,' staff said. 'I think something else is going on.'

As time went on, more and more of the residents took their places at the wall. The village grew as people added their own homes and loved ones. But with so many newcomers, it became evident that they needed rules and called a village council. Chairman Murray used his strong baritone to calm things when the debate overheated. All of them defended the rights of their own loved ones against the rest. Curiously, no one felt it right to give precedence to their families over 'real life' residents of the ward and that became the first rule.

Then they had to decide what to accept as real. They all knew that their physical bodies were seated facing the wall. Yet if they were asked, they'd have said they were in the village hall. But their families were part of them as well. Miss Collins's claim pointed out the problem. She swore she'd seen Lila's son stealing apples from behind Mr Wilson's shop, when no one else was watching, and wanted him punished.

The let's-you-and-him-fight situation was enough. They set out a second rule – that secondary personalities, as they were referred to, couldn't act unless their principals were present. They could no longer cause offence unless it was directly intended.

The third rule applied to principles. They wanted to change their projections sometimes, but were hesitant about disturbing the others. They'd like to visit different times of their lives publicly, not just in the privacy of their 'own homes'.

'I'll show you what I mean,' Vera said. She became a nine year old, speaking and acting as one. Lila humoured her, tossing back a ball Vera threw. Then Vera reverted to the projection of the twenty-year-old she used. 'You could all recognize me, couldn't you?' she asked, and received nods from all. 'If I do it at home, why not here? If it doesn't interfere with what you're doing, is there any harm?'

Everyone liked the new freedom. To prove it, they adjusted themselves to suit their moods. Some appeared in period dress, while others wore the latest fashions to enhance the effect. But no matter what time they chose, the other principals could recognize them.

Everyone felt happier than they had in years. Mr Wilson noted that he'd pushed back the ravages of ageing and disease in his 'ward' body, and others found the same was true of them. On that happy note, they adjourned to a picnic on the village green.

For staff members, administering the ward was easier as patients became more tractable. As long as one person was left 'on duty', as the old folks referred to it, there were no incidents.

The change was so gradual that it took an outsider to see it. The trustees decreed experimentally that the ward would have an occupational therapist twice a week, to bring new interest into what were assumed to be very dull lives. Fresh from training, Karen brought sure-to-please items. In the trolley, she had plastic string and bases for baskets; mortar, tiles, and forms for ashtrays; wool, large needles, and hopsacking for embroidering cushions; and several pads of art paper and felt tip pens.

She walked lightly to the group and surveyed them a moment. They were doing nothing that she could discern. Clearing her throat, she began, 'Hello. I'm Karen, your new occupational therapist. I've brought some things I'm sure you'll be interested in, but if there's something I don't have in my trolley, just tell me and I'll try to get it for you.' Her voice gradually ran down as she realized that none of them were paying the least bit of attention.

She tried a different tactic and reached over to touch the nearest one on the shoulder. 'Hello, dear, I'm Karen. And what's your name, dear?'

Vera sternly shushed her and resumed her contemplation.

Staff told Karen all about the wall. They'd been at it for over fourteen months. She advised the occupational therapist never to get between it and the patients or they'd all regret the consequences. Karen tried a few more tricks to interest the chronically indifferent, but nothing worked.

Dismayed, she asked her uncle on the board for funds to decorate the ward. The first thing she wanted was some wallpaper . . .

WARMTH
Tim Niel

There are voices in the next room when Charlie wakes up, even though, as Charlie knows, there's no one there. Charlie, they say, and then they mutter incomprehensibly, Charlie. Charlie lies still, holds his breath, the way he used to when his parents listened to see if he was asleep, but he can't hear any more clearly. And he knows, anyway, that it's impossible; he knows he should ignore what must either be the remnants of a dream or the first sign of schizophrenia, but he doesn't know how. Charlie, naked and defenceless, lies in his father's bed, in his father's house, waking there for the fourth morning in a row. Charlie's father's in a mental home; that's why he came. Charlie lies naked, head and shoulders aching, and wishes he hadn't left his pyjamas at home, and he lies awkwardly sprawled like a pavement suicide. Charlie, says one of the voices, a little more quietly, Charlie – and then a long sentence, nonsense, commenting unpleasantly – Charlie can tell by the tone of voice – on Charlie, and on his unfortunate ancestry, and on his lack of an interesting future. Charlie lifts his head from the pillow slightly and nods in agreement, in complete concurrence, and the voices stop. It was a dream then; and now I'm awake. It's hot and humid, and my father's been out of his mind for a week.

In the bathroom Charlie stands over the sink, cleaning his teeth, legs still shaky with sleep, his eyes half shut, and he wonders what makes people mad. Somebody once said hormones: someone said something once to Charlie, over a pint, in the days when Charlie and madness were unrelated to each other, that it had something to do with a hormonal imbalance, but Charlie hadn't believed it then and doesn't now, and thinks something must have happened to his father. God knows what; something of apparent insignificance. In the mirror Charlie's mouth foams with toothpaste, and he thinks, rinsing out his mouth, I could pass for rabid, woof woof, barking mad. Drying his face, Charlie rolls up the bathroom blind. Sunlight and Charlie's skin intersect. Hot, thinks Charlie, hot hot, muttering to himself, and he goes downstairs. It's as messy as it was the night before. Charlie picks his way towards the kitchen, stepping over discarded overcoats, spilt tea, and paperwork, and stops off in the sitting room to switch off the television, which he'd left on all night for company.

In the kitchen, eating cornflakes and drinking coffee, Charlie, dismayed, considers the possibility that insanity is genetic. For a minute Charlie contemplates his future wife, whom he still hasn't met, and imagines her, her hands over her mouth, cowering against a wall whilst his brain boils over and he breaks things. But his father isn't like that; he's horribly placid, silent, unmoving, as though mind and body had been surgically separated. Auto-lobotomized, every morning nurses drape his father over a chair and leave him to it, no therapy and as yet no drugs. Presumably to see if he's just having a holiday and will come home of his own accord. Charlie knows he won't. His father's condition reeks both of incontinence and finality. Charlie's father's gone to stay.

Charlie looks down at the empty cup and bowl and runs a hand over his jaw. Normally he shaves every two days, but today, for the first time since the day of his arrival, the doctor has agreed to allow him to see his father, so, today, even though he'd shaved the day before, he will shave again, and he stands, re-knots the loosening belt of his dressing gown, and goes upstairs with mild panic in his belly and head, of a sort that he has previously experienced only before job interviews.

Charlie listens to the water pouring, waiting until it changes its note: it's pouring hot. He puts the plug in and looks at himself in the mirror, and tries several expressions, like an actor. He looks haggard and the stubble casts a faint and dirty shadow across the lower half of his face; but, worse, whatever expression he tries, a sort of grief underlies them all, and Charlie can't see how anyone else could fail to notice, how in particular the psychiatrists could miss it. It's their job after all; and Charlie soaps his face, applies shaving foam, and shaves – long strokes, not thorough, but rough, as though he could remove the layer of skin in which the expression resides. Small pinpricks of blood appear in the razor's wake, and when Charlie rinses the last streaks of foam away the grief's still there. There are shadows underneath his eyes and from there the grief recedes slightly, sinks back, and remains somehow still visible, and to hide it he would need not make-up, Charlie knows, but a mask.

Dressed in his dirty clothes, Charlie sits on the bed and dials the phone number of his office. Through the bedroom window he can see the houses opposite, on the other side of the crescent, and he looks at their windows, some of the curtains still drawn, whilst listening to the ringing tone. When it stops, Charlie doesn't wait for the voice at the other end. 'Martin, please,' he says. 'It's Charlie,' and there's no reply. He or she must know, and doesn't want to talk about it, and Charlie sits and waits while the line whispers until his boss picks up the phone. 'Charlie,' says the voice. 'They're letting me see him today,' Charlie says, and then he listens dimly until he hears a question too simple to misunderstand. 'Early next week,' he says, 'a few more days.' And he listens a little more, and then he says goodbye and hears the buzz and hangs up, obscurely afraid that even in so short a conversation he might have made mistakes, offended or embarrassed, and he stands up and moves a little closer to the window.

Across the crescent, in the morning heat, the other houses appear hazy, as though they had been shot in soft focus, as though the pupils of Charlie's eyes had allowed themselves to become sentimental. Charlie can feel himself beginning to sweat, the uncomfortable prickling of the skin of his legs inside his woollen suit trousers. Charlie momentarily experiences an urge to smash something, and he examines it more closely until he knows, picking up the car keys on the hall table, that the thing he wishes to smash is himself or possibly his father. Charlie can't tell the difference between the two and he realizes that the grief beneath the skin of his face is his father's, is Charlie's likeness, is something to do with the face they both share. Even though they look nothing like each other. The front door slams behind him, and Charlie rests a hand on the car's hot roof – tired.

'Mr Peterson?' says the doctor. 'Mr Peterson.'

'I'm sorry,' says Charlie. The doctor, as discreetly as possible, looks Charlie up and down, once, twice. But in recent times the doctor has been discreet only with the insane and so Charlie notices, and remembers how creased his suit is – rumpled, dark at the armpits – and how dirty his shirt is. Charlie looks back at the doctor, whose face is professionally sympathetic. 'You were saying?'

'I was asking how you felt yourself, Mr Peterson,' says the doctor. 'A great many people find this sort thing hard to take.' He pauses. 'To be frank, you look more than somewhat unsettled.'

'Didn't have time,' Charlie mumbles.

'I beg your pardon?'

'I said I didn't have time,' says Charlie, more clearly. 'When I heard I left home in a hurry, I didn't stop to pack properly. I've been wearing this suit for five days now. And this shirt. I'll wash it tonight.'

'Were you able to take time off work?'

'I informed my employers, yes,' says Charlie, 'they know.'

'What precisely did you tell them?'

'I told them that my father was seriously ill.'

'Not insane?'

'Should I have told them that?'

'I'm sorry. It was wrong of me to have used the word.'

'That wasn't what I meant,' Charlie says, leaning forward

a little, resting an elbow – greasy – on the doctor's desk. 'Should I have told them?'

'It's up to you.'

'All right,' Charlie sits back. The doctor clears his throat.

'How long can you stay?'

'A couple of hours, I suppose,' says Charlie. 'I've phone calls to make, people to see. Bills to pay. He hadn't paid any bills for six months.'

'I meant how long can you stay in the area. And can you afford to pay that much money?'

'It's not that much. I don't think he'd been using any heat or light. It's hardly more than standing charges. And he never used the telephone anyway.'

'That's interesting.'

'Why?'

'It suggests that this attack had been building up for some time.'

'He was always frugal.'

'So frugal that he wouldn't switch a light on?'

'Not during daytime – I'm sorry, how stupid. I mean, not until after lighting-up time.'

'For the streetlamps?'

'Yes.'

'Didn't you think that was a little strange?'

'It was just how he was, doctor. He had an explanation, sort of. He said – used to say – that that was when the experts thought it would be dark. And that since their opinion on this particular matter was printed daily in the newspapers, you might as well take advantage of it.'

'What did you think of that?'

'I thought it was a little irritating.'

'Just irritating?'

'Yes. I thought it was irritating, but logical enough, so far as it went.'

'Why do you say logical?'

'Because you're trying to say he was mad then, which he wasn't.'

'There's no need to shout, Mr Peterson,' says the doctor.

'I'm trying to understand what's happened to your father.' They sit and look at each other. Charlie listens to their breathing, loud in the glassed-in compartment, and scratches his shoulder, and then looks away through the glass at his father slumped in an easy-chair – a modern one, but too well-used, pissed and shat on too many times to be comfortable. His father's head doesn't move.

'I'm sorry,' says Charlie, still looking away.

'I understand,' says the doctor, a useful lie that doesn't fool Charlie for a moment.

'He was short of money when he was young,' Charlie says, 'and he never got out of the habit.'

'Why do you think that was?'

'He didn't trust money.' Charlie turns back to the doctor. 'And he knew however well he was paid, he was still only an employee, and he didn't trust employers either. As a group.'

'Would you describe his distrust of employers as intense?'

'To be honest, doctor, I'd probably describe his distrust of employers as sensible.'

'But did it obsess him?'

'He didn't talk about it often, but everyone in the family was well aware of his views.'

'By which you mean what?'

'Pretty much what I say.'

'I'm trying to help, Mr Peterson.'

'You're doing a fucking poor job,' says Charlie, and then sits staring at the floor at first, feeling trapped, as though in a courtroom interrogation he had admitted his own guilt; and then shamed, because he had accused, and because the accusation was too direct, and because the doctor would dislike him now and Charlie cares about that sort of thing. 'I'm sorry,' says Charlie. 'I didn't mean that. I didn't mean that at all.'

'It's all right,' says the doctor. 'We can stop if you like.'

'No,' says Charlie. 'Can I just see him?'

'In a little while. It would be better if you calmed down yourself before you thought about seeing him.'

'You're quite right.' Charlie nods. 'I'll take my jacket off, it's hot.' And he does so, and sits in his stained shirt like a child home from school.

'Will you be all right if I ask a few more questions?'

'I'll be fine.'

'What would you say your father was like?'

'He was a shy man,' says Charlie straightaway and regrets it as instantly.

'Shy?'

'Not much in company, not the party's life and soul.'

'Unemotional, would you say?'

'Not at all. He was one of the few men I've ever seen cry.'

'When was that?'

'When my younger brother was killed. Hit-and-run-driver.' The doctor's pen begins to scratch across his pad. 'And when mother died, he cried then as well.'

'Any other times?'

'Whenever I left home. He used to cry then.'

'Was he frequently depressed?'

'I suppose, after my mother and brother died, yes. I felt guilty, living so far away. He had no other family.'

'Friends?'

'Some. Not close, I suppose.'

'He was retired?'

'He was sacked, two years ago.'

'Why?'

'Poor sales performance.'

'And how were things financially after that?'

'Not at all bad. They gave him full pension. He was only two and a half years short of retirement anyway. And he'd been with the company thirty years. It was the least they could do. Full pension and severance pay. He wasn't short of money.' The doctor continues to make notes for a while, saying nothing, and then puts his pen down and sits back, crossing his legs. Charlie watches him. Sweat runs down his side beneath his shirt, and he looks at the doctor's face and thinks it's young.

'I expect all of these things were contributory factors, Mr

Peterson,' the doctor says, and Charlie, expressionless, nods. 'It'll do for the moment. If anything else comes up, we'll call you.'

'Yes.'

'Is there anything you'd like to ask me?'

'How long do you think it'll take?'

'For what?'

'For a cure.'

'Well.' He picks up his pen again. 'I'm not sure, not at all sure, that we can talk in terms of a cure, Mr Peterson.'

'I don't want him to stay here.'

'Mr Peterson, I very much doubt that you'd have the time or the money to take care of him. We could have him moved somewhere closer to your own home, if you like, there'd be no problem with that.' Charlie says nothing. 'As to the question of a cure, Mr Peterson, I'm afraid I have to be frank. Your father doesn't respond at the moment to any stimuli at all. We'll try some drugs, of course, but really, in your father's case, I can't hold out much hope. Of course, there's always a chance. Something may well happen.' Charlie looks out of the compartment again. In a distant corner a male nurse bends over another, apparently comatose, patient, with a glass of water. Parting the patient's lips with his fingers, he pours the water between them, closes the mouth, and gently massages; and the patient turns his head. Water dribbles down his shirt.

'So it's not likely he'll be cured.'

'I don't want to depress you, Mr Peterson. In these cases there's usually either a relatively swift recovery – a matter of weeks, a couple of months – or none at all.' Charlie hears a click as the doctor puts his pen down once again. 'I asked a few minutes ago how long you'd be able to stay in the area,' he says. 'Do you know?' Charlie shakes his head and half-shrugs.

'I don't really know,' he says, so quietly that the doctor turns his head behind Charlie to hear better. 'I'll have to phone my office. I don't suppose they'll let me have long.'

'You've given us your home address and phone number?'

'No,' says Charlie, 'I haven't. Only his.' But it's not his any longer. It's Charlie's, by default, or no one's. The doctor slides a card and his pen across the table, and reaches over and taps Charlie on the shoulder. Charlie turns.

'Could you?' asks the doctor. 'Home address and number.' He rests his forefinger on the card for a second. 'In case your office calls you back quite suddenly.' Charlie picks up and pen and begins to write.

'Thank you for the excuse,' Charlie says. 'Do a lot of relatives just leave?'

'Quite a few, I'm afraid.'

'I won't,' says Charlie. 'He's my father.'

'Yes, of course.' The doctor picks up the card and reads it over. 'Nice part of the country.'

'Is it?'

'So I've heard.'

'I've never noticed. He would've.'

'You can go and see him now, Mr Peterson, if you like. Then go home,' he says, as they stand up, reaching out his hand to shake Charlie's, 'and get some sleep. You look as though you need it.' Charlie fumbles with his jacket.

'Thank you for everything you've done.'

'Thank you for coming in to speak with us.' Charlie nods and smiles thinly, and briefly, and turns and opens the door. 'Goodbye,' says Charlie, over his shoulder, and walks towards his father, who sits in the same position, and who isn't his father at all, not anymore.

There's a chair opposite his father's, about three feet away, unoccupied. Charlie sits in it and looks across. It's a thin, empty face, pouched underneath the eyes, pale and sunless, and there's not the slightest sign of recognition. It reminds Charlie of a candid snap, one of those pictures in which someone's caught when their face isn't arranged. 'Hello, daddy,' says Charlie; there's no answer, of course. 'How are you?' The lower lip, wet, trembles slightly, and for a second Charlie thinks he might reply, but it's nothing, as though a leaf moved in the breeze. Charlie reaches forward and takes his father's hand, and looks at the floor. He wonders what else to say, but there's nothing. Everything Charlie can think of seems trite, or pointless, and there's no more family to talk about, only graves. Charlie can't ask what his father does all day because he knows the answer, and because he knows he won't receive one. 'I've been keeping an eye on the house,' he says. 'I'll go and pay the bills this afternoon.' Charlie looks up at the face again and for a second he wants to ask his father where he is and what it's like. Somewhere tideless; all one colour; featureless and hot, not like a holiday at all. Charlie's father's brain ticks over quietly, or stalls somewhere in the past in a memory perhaps, and Charlie, in the end, can't stand the solitude and he puts his father's hand back in his lap and gets to his feet, and his face drifts close to his father's, and he smells him, unwashed and rotten. 'I'll be in tomorrow,' he says, quietly. Then Charlie goes away.

Charlie sits in the car with the engine running at the hospital exit for some time – five minutes, perhaps, or ten; his watch has stopped but he doesn't look at it. Charlie looks straight ahead through the windscreen. The hospital is at the city's edge on a slight rise, and the city lies flat, like something spilt and spreading, below him. It shimmers gently, like the mirages Charlie has seen in cinemas – an imitation of a place to live. Still looking, Charlie loosens his tie and removes his jacket and places it on the passenger seat. Charlie shakes his head and puts his hands on the steering wheel. Charlie knows the city, its streets, its arterial roads, its parks and green places, quite well, but sitting here there's nothing he recognizes, no landmark he knows from such a distance. There are places he worked in when he was a teenager and as a young adult, and somewhere there's the house where he was brought up, and walking the streets there are probably a few faces and names that he might recognize, but not from here.

Charlie drops a hand to the handbrake and checks over his shoulder for traffic but when he tries to move off the car, idling too long, barks twice and dies. Charlie puts the handbrake back on and sits, not panicked any more, but filled with a hot deadness, like an urge to vomit or to cry.

In the Post Office later that afternoon there's a small queue, and Charlie stands with his jacket draped over his arm, holding a sheaf of his father's unpaid bills. He has placed them in order – the oldest is dated sometime last summer, a month after his most recent visit more than a year ago, not six months as he had told the doctor, and these are only the electricity bills. Charlie can't remember if gas bills can be paid at Post Offices or not, his own flat is entirely electric, and he has added up the bills and they come to somewhat more than six hundred pounds. Much more than Charlie had expected, and so it appears that his father's habits had fallen apart – lights in the house left on, night and day, radiators running even in summer. People shuffle up to the service counter and purchase stamps and postal orders, address and post their envelopes, and leave; and at last Charlie slides the bills underneath the little window and speaks into the plastic grille. 'I've come to pay these,' he says.

The clerk riffles through them, sighs, and scratches her neck and scalp. 'Dear dear,' she says. 'Bit late, aren't we?' Charlie shrugs. 'I expect we'll've tried to collect on these already.' Charlie stands and can't think of anything to say, embarrassed, and can only think that her accent's wrong, mild and southern, like his own these days.

'They're not mine,' Charlie says.

'Are you sure they've not been paid?'

'They're an elderly relative's,' Charlie says. 'I don't think so.'

'Gone a bit soft, have they?' she says, smiling, jotting down the figures and totting them up.

'Yes,' says Charlie, horrified. He waits and watches, red in the face.

'Six hundred and twenty-three pounds and twenty-seven pence,' she says. Charlie gets out his cheque book and pen.

'That'll have to be thirteen separate cheques,' she says. Charlie nods, oddly breathless, and begins to write.

'I'd be surprised if there's not a payments scheme set up,' she says. 'The monthly instalments.' Charlie shakes his head. 'At least for the older ones.'

'They weren't paid,' says Charlie. 'I know. He always kept receipts.'

'But if he'd gone a bit soft . . .'

'There were letters complaining about them.'

'Not opened?'

'No.'

'Oh dear. They get like that, don't they? How old is he?'

'Fifty-eight,' says Charlie.

'That's young,' she says. Charlie says nothing, passing her his cheque card and the first few cheques. She begins to scribble the cheque card number on the backs of the cheques, and Charlie continues to write, and he begins to feel pressed for time, urgent, suffocated. She hums and shakes her head, and Charlie thinks, she'll gossip about it later. His father, nobody she ever knew. Charlie scribbles the last cheque and passes it underneath the glass.

'I'm fifty-three myself,' she says, sliding the cheque card back. 'I'll be off the same way myself soon, I expect. Dreadful.' She stamps the bill and tears off the receipt. 'Thank you very much,' she says. Charlie stuffs the cheque book, card and receipt into his hip pocket and nods at her, faintly aware that his mouth's open and that he must look an idiot, and he turns and hurries off without saying anything. 'You've left your pen,' she shouts when he's in the doorway, 'Mr Peterson!' But Charlie doesn't stop. He just thinks, she knows my name. She must've read it on the cheques.

There's something Charlie has to do, but he doesn't know what it is yet. Driving past the last street of tenements before the left turn to his father's semi-detached, it's still light. Charlie had forgotten how early in the year the days get long, up here, and now he thinks, glancing at his stopped watch, it must be getting on for six and not a sign of dusk. He turns to the left without using his indicator and someone sounds their horn behind him, but Charlie doesn't really hear. Charlie parks the car behind his father's, and when he gets out there's someone, a man, looking over the hedge, white hair scraped carefully across his scalp, neat eyes, slightly reddened at the rim. The next door neighbour. Charlie fumbles for the name. 'Evening, Mr Leckie,' he says.

'Szuberlak,' the man says. 'The Leckies moved out three years gone.'

'Oh,' says Charlie. 'I'm sorry.'

'That's all right. Just tidying up, then?' Charlie nods.

'It was me found him,' says Szuberlak, presumably standing on his toes, because now his chin's visible.

'Oh?' says Charlie.

'That's right. He was just sitting in the car, half in and out.'

'Of the car?'

'Of the drive.' It's not a drive, Charlie thinks, it's just a parking space, gravel and cement. Not a drive at all.

'He was crying. I couldn't get him to stop, and he wouldn't talk either.'

'He's stopped now.'

'Oh, you been to see him, then?'

'Yes.'

'How's he doing?' Charlie stands, his jacket over his arm, the car door still open, and wonders what to say, and blushes slowly.

'He's quiet now,' Charlie says, and thinks of the face, not quiet but simply unoccupied.

'That's good,' says Szuberlak, and Charlie nods again and Szuberlak's chin sinks behind the hedge.

'Nice place,' says Szuberlak's voice, slightly muffled by the carefully cropped leaves.

'What, my father's house?'

'Naw, the crescent,' says Szuberlak. 'Never thought I'd get a place as nice, not me. I'm an immigrant.'

'Oh.'

'From Poland. Kraków. Been here thirty years, though.' Szuberlak chuckles, throaty. 'Speak better English than any Irishman.' He falls silent and studies Charlie across the hedgetop, and seems to expect a reply.

'Well done,' says Charlie, smiling like a machine, and Szuberlak's eyebrows crease and Charlie sees that he's offended him. 'I'm sorry,' he says. 'I'm very tired.' Szuberlak's eyebrows settle down.

'Well,' he says. 'Give us a knock if you want a cup of tea.'

'Thanks,' says Charlie. 'I will.' He shuts the car door.

'Night,' says Szuberlak behind him and Charlie turns round, dropping the car keys, to reply but Szuberlak's gone; Charlie can hear his feet trudging up the side passage and his back door open and close, and Charlie bends down and picks up the keys and puts them in his pocket, and leaves the car unlocked.

The house is quiet and stifled because Charlie had closed all the windows before he left. In the kitchen he opens one and puts the kettle on, and stands there listening as it begins to hiss, and then he remembers what Szuberlak had said and fetches dustbin bags from the cupboard under the sink. Charlie throws his jacket down on the hall table, over the telephone, and takes the bags into the sitting room, and begins to fill one with food and papers and discarded tissues and tins, and when it's finished and the sitting room looks if not cleaner at least a little less like a midden he goes upstairs although he hadn't planned to and continues, listening to the kettle whistle in the kitchen. It'll boil dry. Charlie fills two sacks and wanders into a bedroom and strips the bed, wondering briefly why it was made at all, and then goes into the bedroom he's been using and strips that bed as well, throwing the sheets into a linen basket; and then the bathroom. There's a sponge on the side of the bath and he gives the mirror a cursory wipe, and all the time he's half aware that he's speeding up, working faster, accelerating towards what? A sort of escape velocity; and then he goes downstairs, carrying the dustbin bags and leaves them in the hall, and in the kitchen he turns the kettle off. Then he fetches the plates and cups from the sitting room, gathers up the crocks from the kitchen table, and in the sink he washes them all, approximate and careless, feverish and quick. Charlie closes the kitchen window and opens the sink cupboard and reaches in and turns off the stopcock. He ties up the dustbin bags at the neck, and in the cupboard under the stairs he turns off the electricity and gas. In the sitting room, in the desk, he finds an envelope and puts the keys in, and on the front he writes his address and back soon and signs it – Charlie Peterson; and then, out of the front door, with the sacks, and he dumps them beside the streetlight. Then Charlie goes back in for the envelope, and he steps out, closes the door and listens as it latches, and creeps round as quietly as possible to drop the envelope through Szuberlak's front door. And then Charlie runs back to his car and remembers that his jacket's still on the hall table but it's empty; his cheque book and card are still in his trouser pocket and so's his wallet, so it doesn't matter. Charlie gets into the car, slips the key in and turns it, and reverses, and Szuberlak's front door opens and Szuberlak comes out, waving the envelope and mouthing something and looking displeased. And Charlie waves back and smiles, feverish and afraid, and drives away.

Charlie follows streetsigns out through the city centre and there's hardly any traffic. His watch says it's half past two and Charlie switches the radio on and drives, foot down and in fourth when at all possible, until he's on the motorway and passing signs that say A7 Carlisle and the South, and it's getting dark at last and Charlie's breaths begin to come longer and he thinks, overtaking a restaurant at ninety-five miles an hour, it's all right Charlie. It's all right Charlie, a letter'll do.

BEST FRIENDS
Jennifer Murray

I had to stop and pick up the scissors because I dropped them from the top of the tree, but I was catching her up easy as anything. Her head was rolling about and her long plaits were doing a ragdoll dance down her back.

She can't run for toffee. I was laughing inside, but I was mad with her too. The branches cracked under my feet. I was so near now I could hear her blubbering. I caught her, and she crouched down and blew her nose. When Josephine blows her nose it sounds like a big let off. She does it in class, and everyone in the back row laughs. It sounded funny in the woods, all quiet after.

She said, 'Susan's never going to be your best friend now.'

'Your skirt's stuck up your behind again,' I said. She made me mad saying that about Susan.

'She can't do everything. See.'

'Oh, yes, she can,' I said, and I snipped the scissors in the air. She didn't move. She knew what I was going to do.

'You promised,' I said.

The trouble started when Josephine said, 'Oh yeah, pooh,' to Susan, and walked off. Susan said she could fly. She said she could fly off the top of the school roof. So when Josephine said, 'Oh yeah, pooh,' and everybody who sits in the back row laughed, Susan got really mad.

She can do anything, Susan. She's really clever. She can do a backwards somersault so her head comes out through her legs, and then wave. She sits in the back row in the corner by the window, and I'm going to be her best friend.

Susan was so mad after Josephine walked off, she made me cry. I didn't let her see though. She said she only came round my house because I live next door to her. Everybody laughed at me then, and walked off after her. It's horrible being friends with two girls who hate each other. Well, I'm not really friends with Josephine, I just have to be.

Nobody likes Josephine, I think her mum does a bit. People stare at her in the street because her head shakes all the time, and she's blind as a bat nearly. She looks like my white mouse Snowy. People think I'm funny because I'm with her. I know they do. I hate her. She's got a stupid doll with a stupid name called Isobella.

My mum says there but for the grace of God, and never to point or poke fun at those less fortunate than ourselves. That's why I have to be friends with Josephine, apart from she's always got some chocolate in her pocket, and I wish her mum was my mum. My mum says her mum didn't want an albino. She wanted a normal little girl, which is true because when I stay round Josephine's her mum kisses me goodnight just like she does Josephine. Better.

I think Josephine could at least say please and thank you considering everything I do for her and I'm her only friend – not really friends, I just have to be. And I always ask nicely if I want a bit of chocolate off her. Always one piece at a time too. She's thick. Thick as her glasses. The holes in her nose touch the chocolate nearly when she takes the silver paper off, she won't let me do it, and sometimes her mum follows her to school in the morning, hiding behind bushes and things to see if we're bullying her. We seen her. She's got a nice bedroom.

I had to wait ages and ages before Susan came through our hedge again, still chewing from teatime. That's when she said I could be her best friend if I wanted, and what I had to do, I had to help her get Josephine into the woods at the back of our garden and cut off one of her plaits.

My mum said Josephine's mum was scared if she had another baby it would come out like Josephine. That's how she got a bedroom all by herself. I have to share mine with my big sister because my mum had to have five girls before my little brother popped out. He was a present for my dad. He's the boy so he's got his own room. My big sister's got bosoms now. She tries to hide them but I can see. Budding breasts, that's what my dad calls them. When she's fast asleep she chews and chews the sheet till no more will fit in her mouth. I have to get up every night after, and pull and pull till it all comes out. I hate him. I'm going to cut mine off when they start budding.

At first when Susan said to me about cutting it off, I told her I wasn't allowed in the woods except for if I could still see our fence. We're not allowed after a man asked me once and my next sister down from me to pick some bluebells with him. I said, 'No, but thank you for asking,' and we ran off. My mum said that was the right thing to do. She said he was a sick man, but he seemed all right, smiling and pedalling on his bicycle. My dad said he would kill me if we went in the woods again.

After I said to Susan about not being allowed, she said, 'Do you want to be my best friend or don't you?' so I said, 'Yes.' I said, 'Snowy's going to have her babies soon. You can come and watch if you like.' Susan said we had to trick Josephine into the woods. I had to tell her to come and watch Susan flying from the top of a big tree.

'All right,' I said. I was trying not to be too happy. Then I said, 'She better not say "Oh yeah, pooh" this time, or else.' Susan didn't say anything, only to bring my mum's big dressmaking scissors.

I said to Susan, was everybody in the back row coming to watch her fly too, and she looked at me in a funny way.

'Don't be pathetic.'

I looked so she couldn't see my face, but after I knew what she meant. She meant I was going to be her best friend. It was going to be just me and her, just us two by ourselves.

Josephine got away from me, but I caught up with her again easily and a big sob came out of her. I wouldn't let her go this time.

'You think a lot of your hair, don't you,' I said. She can

sit on it, and she has never ever had it cut. Not even a little bit. She told me once it would fetch a fortune if she sold it, hair her colour that's natural. It's pure white. Susan said it came out of a bottle, and everybody laughed. But it's not true, it grows out of her head, you can tell.

All of a sudden I had a good idea. 'How much are your plaits worth?' I said.

'They're not for sale.'

I was thinking, if I cut both plaits off near the top I could get a lot of money for Susan. I've got a shoe box at home from my new sandals and it's still got the tissue paper in. I could wrap the plaits up nicely so someone will pay a lot for them.

'You'll never be best friends with her now,' Josephine said.

'Stop saying that. Stop it,' I said.

'It's true.'

'She said she was going to be my best friend, so she is. And don't look at me like that.' There was a milky green bubble coming in and out of her nose. I twisted one of the plaits, and the pink skin where the hairs grew came up like goose flesh. There were red marks where she tried to get away from me.

'Don't be pathetic,' I said. She pulled away from me. She kept pulling away from me so I couldn't do it. I was getting worried about being in the woods now. Josephine must have known what I was thinking because she said, 'If you cut my plaits I'll tell your dad where you've been.'

'You better not,' I said, but I was worried my dad would kill me if he found out.

I was worried as well because I was going to tell a fib to Susan. My mouse Snowy had her babies. It was in the middle of the night so we missed it. I didn't dare tell Susan. So I thought, if she asks I'll tell her Snowy's due any day now. That's what I'll say. It's not really a lie, not like saying she hasn't had her babies yet. Anyway I've still got two under my bed if she wants to see them.

I counted seven altogether, I think it was. They were

shiney pale pink and all stuck together. My mum said I had to get rid of them so I did. She said she had enough animals in the house already. She meant me and my sisters, I know, because we haven't got a dog or anything.

I put them down the toilet. Two of them came unstuck and bobbed up on top of the water, so I had to wait till the toilet filled up again. I let my little brother try the second time because he came to watch and he wanted to. He's really fat; I think he was born with elastic bands round his arms and legs. I had to help him stand on the edge of the toilet seat and he looked down inside and I told him when to push the handle. When the water was still coming out I said, hands together eyes closed, and I said a prayer. He nearly fell in, but it was all right because my dad was out. At the end I pushed the handle again exactly on amen.

When we opened our eyes, we saw the two little babies still bobbing about. I said to my brother to get down, and I went downstairs to the dining room to fetch a big spoon and I fished them out and saved them in our red plastic soap box. They didn't move.

Susan hasn't asked me about them yet. But I know everything will be all right if I can get the plaits and make them look nice in the tissue paper in the shoe box and give them to her.

At first when we got her to the woods, Josephine wouldn't climb up the tree. She said she would watch Susan from the bottom. 'Because you can't climb,' I said. It's true. She says help when she's stuck in gym. In France if you drown you have to say *au secours*. It's stupid.

'I won't fly if you don't come up the top with me,' Susan said to Josephine.

In the end we all climbed up the tree. I had my mum's scissors in my knickers so Josephine couldn't see. I could tell she was scared but she really wanted to see Susan fly, and so did I. Josephine stopped on a branch halfway up. 'Fly from here,' she said.

'No,' said Susan. 'We got to go higher.'

We kept climbing higher and higher. The scissors poked

me. Then Susan stopped, and we all stopped. I was in the middle.

'I'll fly if you let us cut off one of your plaits,' Susan said.

She looked at me and I looked in my knickers and found the scissors and showed them so Josephine could see. I'm not really sure but I think Josephine was going to say, 'Oh yeah, pooh!' again. I'm not sure though.

She said, 'You fly first, and then I'll let you.'

I was really happy. 'You'll let us cut off one of your plaits?' I said.

'Susan's got to fly first.'

'No,' said Susan. 'She cuts off your plait. Then I fly.'

'You fly first,' said Josephine.

It was stupid. I grabbed one of her plaits, and I had the scissors in my other hand. She started to wriggle about and she pushed me. I got a funny taste in my mouth because we were a long way up. Susan stood up tall and said to Josephine, 'Don't you dare do that. Don't you ever dare push her again.'

It was all quiet high in the woods, and I was really, really happy. After a bit, I said to Susan, 'You go first. Go on.' She gave me a funny look I hated. I think she was cross with Josephine.

'Go on,' I said.

'Go on,' Josephine said.

'Go on.'

And I gave her a push.

One good thing, Josephine's too scared to be in the woods alone now. The trees are whispering, and that's why she isn't running away from me any more.

I thought Susan would fly better than that, but it doesn't matter. I still want to be her best friend. At the bottom, after, she didn't move. I twisted both Josephine's plaits hard, and the goose flesh on her head went white and then red. 'I can cut them off now, you said.' I was still scared she would tell my dad I was in the woods. She was crying and crying.

'It's our secret,' I said. 'You mustn't tell him. Stop crying.' There was a horrible smell of warm coming out of her and she was shining all over like my dad. She kept wiping her hands on her skirt.

'If you tell,' I said, 'you'll have to go into a Home, and you'll never see your mummy and daddy again.'

I opened the scissors out really wide.

THE FOX'S NEST
John Cunningham

The bell rang and he answered it because there was no one else in.

A tall man with a bald head, motionless on the step. Then he had held out his hand, 'Hal Clark.' The hand slowly fell. 'You are Mr Fraser?'

This implied that he knew he was talking to Mr Fraser and not to anyone else in the house. Coupled with the offered handshake, the open neck shirt and pullover, the smile, it was unpromising.

'Heard you might do a job for me. A wall to build.' Hal Clark was no longer looking at him, though in his direction.

'A wall?' Eddie said, thinking he was a snoop, or else a fellow trying to work him into a corner. There was a sharp Adam's apple with the black stubble thicker on one side and skin pimpled like chicken flesh.

'In my garden. To hold up a bank.'

Eddie caught his eye. 'Bank of Scotland?'

The fellow laughed, looking puzzled all the same.

'How much?'

'Two pounds an hour.'

He counted how much that would be a week, wondered about signing off, but knew he'd take it just for the work. 'I'm busy. I'll come tomorrow.'

'Ah.' Hal gave him a card on which was written his address. 'Tomorrow then. Tomorrow then, Eddie. Take a thirty-five to the terminus. Whitefield Avenue runs off from there. You can't miss.'

*

It was a row of bungalows with burglar alarms. The distant outline of hills stood against the sky. He could go out there and climb, or just walk among them whenever he liked – an odd feeling.

160 was near the end of the Avenue, different from the others, being two-storeyed and old-fashioned.

I'm smarter than him. Tougher. He saw himself whirling up the bricks.

The house had its own wall, as soon as he'd passed the previous bungalow; a low wall with pillars at intervals that might have supported chains. A dark hedge grew within. He came to a driveway rising steeply to the house. Past it the hedge continued and turned a right angle, dividing 160 from the next house.

He started to go up between the concrete wheel tracks, passing various bushes and a rockery. A path diverged, winding through the rockery to a front door under a tiled porch, but he went on up the drive which rounded the house and curved down to a concrete pool.

As though beside a real pool, Hal and a woman sat in deckchairs. It could have been a tropical island, the blonde woman suntanned. The garden encircled them. Away across it were the hills. He was going down towards them. Hal waved.

'Glad you made it, Eddie. This is Margaret, m'wife.'

'I'm going to make coffee,' she said. 'Like some?' While she was in the house he asked about the wall.

'I'll show you . . .' Hal frowned. 'Sit down.' He might have meant the chair but Eddie sat on the grass. 'I haven't told her about you. No need, eh? Don't want to worry her. You know what they're like.'

She came out with a tray. She was definitely wearing a bikini under a loose coat. She raised her eyebrows. 'Milk and sugar?'

He nodded. 'Two sugars.' Taking the mug he saw that her eyes were mostly green. Her relaxed manner was to make him feel at home, lying back in her chair, not being bothered, making it more fucking one-sided. He drank the coffee quickly and asked to see the job; and when they were alone he asked Hal, 'How did you know?'

'Pal of mine on the staff.'

'Worked with ex-cons before?'

'No.'

He believed it. Hal was a bad liar. And a strange article – now coughing and striding forward to point at the end of the garden. 'I'll give you a hand with the rough stuff,' he said. A bank topped with a straggling hedge was to be squared off. The trees to be uprooted. When the wall was built, the spoil would be thrown behind, levelled and turfed so that the lawn would seem to sweep forward and end – wall and ditch being invisible from the house side. 'I'll get you a spade.'

He brought it from the house along with a builder's line that he pegged out to show where the bank was to be cut, close to the trees.

'Easier to get the trees first,' Eddie said.

Hal walked away.

He started to slice the bank. As the morning passed his hands blistered, stones and roots twisting the spade in his grip.

When she came out and said it was lunch time he considered briefly asking for a cup of tea, sitting for a break and working on, but decided against it.

The kitchen was cool. 'You should be out of the sun for a bit,' she said. He saw a table and chairs outside where they might have sat getting tanned, and watched her putting sliced cucumber and tomato and other things on a dish, her back to him. 'Have a wash,' she said, nodding to the sink. 'The bathroom's . . .' she jerked her head, her hands busy. He was looking at the inside of her thigh. Old enough to be your ma, for Christ's sake.

Hal gave him a can of beer with the meal.

'The haw-haw's my idea,' she was saying in a posh voice, with a laugh. 'Dividing our land from the park, you know,' she added, pointing, the nest of golden hair showing in her armpit.

Later on Hal said he would order cement.
'You'll need a mixer,' Eddie said.
'Mixer? Sure!' Hal grinned, showing long, spaced lower teeth, pretending to shovel.

Cement, sand and gravel came. He had been working there quite a few days.

In the kitchen Hal had a hangover. 'Sit down,' he said between his teeth as Eddie made footprints round the red tile floor. 'Have a coffee. Give a man a break. I'll be with you in a minute.'

Eddie went out. He'd filled the trench with stones the day before, but it seemed advisable to wait for the boss before starting concreting.

To fill in time he had a look at the tools. These were kept mostly under an upturned fibreglass boat in a space between the house and the wall dividing next door's garden. There was a sectional building, stacked as it had been delivered, which would one day house the boat and tools. He took a barrow and two shovels to the tips of sand and gravel and wandered back to the boat.

The trees . . . the axe was blunt and he took the bushman saw. They were the kind of trees that grow on waste ground and these had at one time been trimmed into a hedge; straggly branches had sprung up from the old waist-high stumps. He cut them off where he could get the saw in. The sawdust was damp and greenish, the wood itself yellow and pink, and then brown towards the middle. He'd cleared most of the first tree when he saw the nest in the one beside it. It could hardly be imagined how he'd missed it; now he saw it, it was obvious.

The bird was something special. Glossy, but you could see the fine feathers. The beak could rip into you. The eyes shone – she could have been wired to high voltage. Fascinated, he leant nearer; the feathers moved up and down with her breathing.

She rocketed suddenly past his head with a touch of a

wing or claw. So quick he hadn't seen the wings open. He looked round in time to catch the dipping flight into the next garden.

The eggs lay together in the mud-lined circle, blue patched with chocolate. The door opened and Hal strode towards him, angry. Maybe the hangover.

'What's up?'
'A birdnest.'
'Eh!'
'A fox's nest!'

'Eh!' His eyes showed fright, worsened by the night before, but only for a second. The anger returned, they flushed, his whole face flushed. 'Don't mess me around, son.'

Eddie stood for a while; he controlled a certain space. 'See for yourself.'

Hal shoved out his chin, able to see into the nest without rising on his toes. And after a bit he leant back on the tree, against the forked branch where the nest was. He crossed his legs.

'Just your blacky. No big sweat that.' He paused. 'You're a bit of a joker. Fox's nest.' There was a stare. People would not often look at you; it could have been a mistake for Hal soon dropped his eyes, he shifted off the tree. Looking down he said, 'Listen boy, you're keen to get these trees – we'll do 'em. Only take a day, eh?'

'Not with the bird there.'

'She won't be back.' Hal came to stand close. His sweat smelt. 'Find the axe?' he asked. Eddie stepped back, but Hal wouldn't look up. 'Did you?' he asked again.

'I'm not cutting that one.'
'Start the other end. Okay?'
There was a pause.
'Your axe is blunt,' Eddie said.

'We'll sharpen it. I've a stone up there.' Hal came to life, seemed almost to be going to reach out and touch him. He was humming as they walked, and reached under the boat with a quick swoop for a Carborundum stone.

'You do it,' Eddie said.

Hal leant on the stacked shed sections and rubbed the axe with long slow strokes on the stone that he had wedged against a timber. The sectional shed was the kind they claimed could be put up with a spanner. There was a bag of nuts and bolts, and beside it a light pulley. Eddie picked it up and straightened the thin nylon cords on to the wheels of the pulley blocks.

Hal glanced up. 'That didn't come with the shed. Had it for years.'

'Looks like a toy.'

'Huh! It would lift you no bother. Lift half a ton. I'll use it to lift the roof trusses.' A wire had been looped round a branch hanging over from the next garden. The muscles on Hal's arms poking out of the T-shirt moved slackly as he turned the stone fine-side up and spat. He screwed up his eyes. The axe had a bright crescent round it. 'Here. Feel that.'

Eddie put his finger on the blade. It would have sliced the skin if he'd pressed.

'Start the far end,' Hal was saying. He'd passed the tree with the nest and called back over his shoulder, 'What?'

Eddie repeated, 'She's there.'

Hal paused, but went on, squaring up to the tree at the other end of the line. 'Let's see how tight she sits!' He swung, striking near the root. At the second blow a chip flew. He sweated as he chopped, angry again.

Eventually the tree fell, leaving a six inch stump.

'You should have cut up here,' Eddie said, taking the bushman to the next tree. When he'd cut off the branches he used the three foot stump as a lever. Roots showed as underground heavings, then jerked up through the grass. He chopped through one or two with the spade and dragged the whole thing out, looking up and nodding at Hal. With the stump horizontal, he sawed it clear of the root, the bushman flinging out spurts of sawdust, making a dry ticking as it went back and forward.

When the log bumped on to the turf he stood up and went to see if the bird was sitting.

'That's all the trees I'm cutting,' he said, coming back.

Hal was leaning on the axe. He shifted his weight to stand upright. 'Right then. We'll call it a day.'

Eddie stared. The job –*finito*! Bastard! If he thought . . .

'It's Saturday,' Hal said quickly. 'Nearly dinner time. Not worth an hour's concreting, eh? It's nearly dinner time.'

'Ah. Oh, aye.' Eddie nodded. 'See what you mean. I . . . Margaret said she'd cut my hair. When she's back from the shops. I can start the concrete after dinner, eh? May as well do something, eh?'

'Up to you.'

She was putting food on the table. He and Hal were washing their hands, then taking their places at the table. It occurred to him that everything was right in the house. It was well ordered, perhaps normal for this kind of house. No children, of course, but they'd have fitted in. Completely different. If his family had been in this place the floor would be covered in stuff, Ma wouldn't be able to get about for things in her way, there'd be music, papers on the table.

Hal was shoving him a can of beer.

He pulled the ring and at the same time knocked the can over, a bubbly pool spreading between the plates. He knocked it again, increasing the mess. His hand had operated on its own but he was pleased with the results, jumped up and got a cloth. He lifted plates and wiped the blue formica table top.

'Sorry, sorry!' He wrung the cloth in the sink and wiped the underneath of the wet plates – Hal smiled vaguely when his was done – and rinsed the cloth and wrung it out again. The table was almost dry and smelt slightly of beer and squeezy.

Margaret put out a bowl of salad and a platter of ham. She was wearing a cotton dress and with her movement the shape of her bum was visible. He felt like butting his head against it. He wanted to stretch and laugh.

'Tell me what you've been doing while I've been cleaning this blessed house,' she asked.

'Working,' Hal said.

'We found a nest.'

She smiled, making them a family, friends, workmates, yes a family.

'Should have heard him!' Hal chuckled, opening a can and handing one across. 'Had me going! Kidded on it was a fox's nest!'

She frowned at his laughter.

'Aye,' he spoke through a mouthful, 'blackbird, in the hawthorns. We'll leave her, no problem. If she stays, mind. She'll have a struggle with the cats. Should have taken the gun to them in the spring.'

'Have you got one?' Eddie asked.

'Well, old one. No licence or anything.'

Strange, a gun in the house.

'Crows,' Hal said. 'They take the eggs. Who'd be a bird. But we'll give her a chance, as I said. I was always soft-hearted, eh?' He leant against Margaret, their arms touching.

Eddie had been watching them through half-shut eyes. 'That bird will hatch soon,' he said, and looked out of the window.

'Expert, are you?' Hal asked.

'It's my opinion.'

'You wouldn't see many birds where you're from,' Hal said, his voice dying away.

'Oh? Where?' Margaret asked.

He hesitated, but Hal was not looking at him. 'The jail,' he told her.

'Didn't want to worry you, lass,' Hal said. Foam was running over the top of his glass. He and Margaret looked at each other, both afraid.

He stood out of himself and saw he shouldn't have frightened her, he wished he hadn't.

She said, 'I don't mind at all, of course not. I'm interested. The real prison, you mean?' Neither of them answered.

'I meant where were you from before that, really. Your home.'

'Ah.'

'Could you see out?' she asked, with a high laugh. 'It sounds daft, but I've always wanted to know.'

'I never bothered. Inside, that was your life.'

'I see what you mean.' She'd turned smooth and distant like a woman interviewing someone. 'It must have been difficult when you came out. I mean, getting back to ordinary life. Your family would be . . .'

'Dead,' he said, 'except my two brothers and I don't speak to them.'

'Just so,' Hal said, after a pause. 'I remember the time I was in the army doing my two years. Hard graft then, boy. Guard duty, forty-eight-hour weekends in a dump like Catterick, trussed in uniform and I don't know what all straps like a bloody turkey. You went round at night with a pick handle you were supposed to keep the Russians out with. But all you did was chase sheep! They came off the moor at night looking for scraps in the bins. First time I heard this clatter! Thought it was the attack! Bin rolling at me in the dark with a sheep hanging out!'

'Hal,' Margaret said.

'Three shillings a day, boy.'

'Hal.'

'Mind,' Hal gripped the table, 'it's serious being put away.'

Eddie had his pinky under a can and was revolving it with his other fingers and thumb. Periodically he pressed in the sides, distorting the girl and making a pop.

'Messes up your career,' Hal said. 'I know you learn a trade and that . . .'

'For labourer's wages.'

'You hadn't much luck till I came along.'

'They don't like jailbirds.'

'I'll need to go,' Margaret said.

Hal lifted a can from the floor. 'I'm going to see what's on the box.'

'All right if I start the found?' Eddie asked him, and Hal

nodded. He said to Margaret, 'I'll be out there when you come back. For the hair, you know. If that's okay.'

She smiled and nodded.

He took off his shirt and placed shuttering at the end of his trench. He noted the blackbird on its nest. Margaret had run the car down the drive and he heard it going along the road as he began to shovel. She had seemed less afraid by the time she'd left. There was the possibility that she found having a convict in the house exciting. He frowned and mixed the first batch.

He worked steadily between the mixing site and the trench, enjoying the sun and the work. Halfway along the found he began to be quite tired and slowed down. There was a vague hum in the air, of traffic towards the centre and maybe machines in the fields, and through it, occasionally, he heard the TV. He thought of Hal lying in his chair there, and Margaret, seeming to glide through the shops. In some way he held things together for them, there was an illusion that the well-being of the place depended on him. A bit of plaster had fallen from the side of the house, cracks starting out through the nearby plaster from the patch of bare stonework. He thought it should be fixed. Strange it didn't feel strange.

Just a dream but. A week or two would see the thing finished.

It was getting difficult to work for thinking of the impending haircut. Apparently she'd worked in a salon in town till recently, and in a coat that looked as if there was nothing underneath. He breathed deeply and let it out slowly. The hairdressing salon was real and unreal, like the neat kitchen. Couldn't get a hold of it. A situation maybe like clawing your way into the TV screen, there'd be nothing there.

He began to think he wasn't bothered about having his hair cut, might say he'd changed his mind. There was a lot to be said for the open air. His skin didn't look red in the sunlight, but by the feel of it, was probably burnt. Soon be like the gangs on the roads and building sites, always a gang of them.

Touching occurred during hairdressing, her breasts would touch his back, move across his shoulders. And then the close pressure of the inside of her arms on his head. Immediately his penis was stiff.

But there was a catch somewhere, as if the woman's touch carried a code for his extinguishing. And he went at the barrowing again.

It became obvious that he'd finish the found before the end of the afternoon. That meant they could start to build the wall on Monday.

He made his way across the lawn to the window where the curtain was partly drawn. Hal heaved out of his chair, came over, and Eddie said they would need the blocks for Monday.

'What's the hurry?'

Eddie shrugged.

'There's those trees,' Hal said, glancing at the TV. 'There's the shed.'

'Why don't you order them?'

'It's the weekend!'

'The guy's a friend of yours. Get him before the next race!'

Hal shoved his hands in his pockets and lunged out to the phone.

Eddie watched javelin, and the runners limbering up for the 1500 metres, taking off their tracksuits.

'I used to do a bit of that,' he said when Hal came back.

'First thing Monday.'

He did a warm-up run across the grass and a couple of starts before trundling the barrow to the sand and gravel tips.

'Are you coming?'

The whitening concrete gave off a salty smell. He left it reluctantly and followed her inside.

While she was upstairs his eyes adjusted to the dimness of the kitchen and he rubbed the dirt off his hands at the tap. He heard the TV and wondered how they'd done in the 1500. He fancied doing the sprints again though he'd soon be what they called a veteran. Funny thinking yourself young and being one of the knotty-legged old guys. She came back in a hairdresser's coat, carrying the sort of mirror normally fixed to a wall, and she put it beside the sink, smiling as she placed a chair in front. He had a sliding view of them both in the mirror and scissors and a comb on the draining board as he sat down.

She was testing the water. 'I'll wash it first.' He went to take off his shirt but it was lying outside on the grass. 'Here,' she said, guiding his head under the tap. Water ran down his face and into his mouth. It was turned off, his head pulled up and shampoo massaged into his scalp. 'You've got strong hair,' she said. He had not imagined someone else's touch correctly. Nothing like it. Different world from thinking about it. Her fingers pressed down and he pressed up. 'This is what I use. Birch sap.'

'Ah' – not having known of such stuff. She curved round his back. He was holding the sink, his elbow touching the moving underside of her breast as she worked in the shampoo.

She ran the water again, rinsed his hair and towelled it.

'There,' she said, her hands on his shoulders. Her fingers gripped slightly on his collarbones, the tips just curling over, and he was reaching up. His hand on the back of her neck pulled her over his shoulder and he kissed the side of her mouth.

Her tongue, electric.

He breathed and loosened his hold, turning, and her arms pinned him in the chair, hands gripped the skin of his belly and her head bored into his skull, she bit his cheek.

He jumped loose and grabbed for her but she'd moved back. She made a face and flipped her hand.

'Go away. Go on. Go and shave.'

He took hold of her. Her wrist might have been trapped,

and not lightly held, from the way she seemed to be pulling back, although her arm was curved.

'Forget it,' she said. 'Go on. I'll cut your hair in a minute.'

'Eh?'

'You're going out, aren't you? You can't go like that!' He hadn't moved. 'Use his razor!' she explained, pulling away her arm to point upstairs. 'He's having a bath.'

He crossed the room, nodding to her at the door. On the stairs he wondered how Hal wasn't at the TV, but he was in the bathroom right enough. He opened the door a crack. 'Okay to come in? Margaret said to shave.' He opened the door further. A bath was across his vision, Hal's head sticking out at the left hand end, taps at the right next to a washbasin. The window was fogged up.

'Come in and shut the door. What is it?'

'A shave. Margaret said maybe use your razor.'

Hal peered through the steam.

'She's been washing my hair. Letting it dry just. She'll cut it after.'

'Oh, I see.' Hal was smiling.

'All right – the razor?'

'On you go, son. Better put in a new blade. In the cabinet there.'

He took out a can of foam, the razor and a packet of blades. Wiping the mirror, he saw faint toothmarks on his cheek. It seemed not to matter if Hal had noticed. The chances were even; he was in the game now, the thing was to keep running. He smoothed on foam and started to shave, glancing at the bath which was scummy and full to the overflow. Now and then a yellow toe bobbed up near the taps but mostly there was only the head. The bath was an old one on cast iron claws, long enough for Hal to lie straight.

He gave his face a good rub, took the blade out and put it separately in the cabinet. Hal's foot was poised out of the water, and he reached forward helpfully.

Hal shook his head, jabbed at the hot tap and winced as the sharp bits caught his instep. 'Squeeze in some of that, will you?'

Eddie took a plastic bottle and squirted a jet under the tap. Castles of foam were drifting up the bath as he closed the door.

He didn't know, on his way down. His balls ached, making thought difficult.

She was reading a magazine and put it down when he came in, smiling in a composed way. 'You look a great deal better,' she said briskly.

She started to comb and make a parting. He noticed that he looked like everyone else, like the kind of person he passed in the streets.

She was moving his head with a businesslike touch, using comb and scissors above the ear, the warm touch cooled by the image. He wished she'd finish. He was only a head of hair to her, till she asked, without interrupting her turning out of the comb, 'Were you in prison long?'

'Most of my life.'

'No! Really? You're joking.'

He caught her attention in the mirror.

'I see,' she said.

The thing became inevitable because he was looking into her eyes in the mirror and she was holding his head. The kitchen was quiet except for the blood rushing round in his skull, the silence gathering into intakes of breath. 'I killed a fellow.'

Her eyes darkened and she drew back. One hand was still on his shoulder as her face pulled together round the big eyes. 'Oh my . . .'

The heads were one above the other in the mirror. She had her hand to her mouth, the points of the scissors in front of her eye. The pupil was in the V of the blades; it was up to him in case she jagged herself with the points or something. Nothing sudden.

'Eh . . .' She moved back and he stopped. 'It's all right,' he said to the mirror, 'nothing. It's by.'

'Who?'

'One of my mates actually.' He paused. 'An accident, you know how it is, we were fighting.'

There was silence, and she looked at him.

'Stuck a knife in him.'

She began doing his hair, and at times when he looked up she was frowning.

'Does Hal know?'

He shrugged. 'He never said.'

'Hal's got strong views, you know.' She was pressing heavily with the comb, combing all round and frowning at the hair.

He held his hand to his neck.

She saw him in the mirror, and nodded.

As she was finishing she said, 'You've given me a shock, Eddie. I'll have to think about it.'

'Aye, sure. I'm sorry.'

'I'm annoyed with myself, I should have known.' She started to laugh. 'I was going to say I'm not shocked! What I mean is I'm not outraged. I'm not thinking you're inhuman, it just takes getting used to.'

They were at breakfast on Monday morning, he saw them through the window.

The blocks hadn't come, they would have been beside the sand and gravel. Margaret beckoned, but first he went to see the found. It was hard and true, a pioneer's road. He jumped down and walked on it. 'Spot on,' he said, vaulting back up to the bank where the trees were. He walked wide of the end, but glimpsed that the bird was away. Thinking they must be hatched and she'd gone for food, he went closer. The nest was empty.

It was made of straw and stems woven together and fixed in a fork of branches, still mostly hidden by leaves. He touched the grey plastered inside. It began to feel warm under his finger, light and strong when he moved the branches with slight pressure. An empty house. She wouldn't be back after the burglary.

He strolled towards the kitchen, and as soon as he stepped in saw that Hal had done it. He stayed in the doorway and Margaret looked up; she was going to ask if he was okay, so he told them, 'The eggs are gone.'

Hal pretended not to have heard, buttering a slice of toast.

'What's that you say, boy?'

He repeated, 'The eggs are gone.'

'Empty? Did you look for signs of cats? Did you? Claw marks?' Hal swilled a mouthful of tea as if he had to leave suddenly. The inside of his mouth was seen. He scratched his head. 'Gave her a chance. Gave her a chance. Didn't we?' He had long bones, large hands, head and feet, not much flesh, a skinny guy but heavy. 'Didn't we?'

'Where's the blocks?'

Hal clasped his hands. 'He assured me . . . ,' he started. 'Ah!' It was the tremendous roar of the lorry they heard, reversing up from the road.

Eddie caught it cresting the hill, got the driver's attention and waved him back to as near the work as he could get without leaving the concrete driveway, beside the sand, although because of the room taken up by it and the gravel, the blocks would spill on to the grass.

He held up his hand, went forward and pulled the latch on the tailgate and signalled the driver to tip. The body of the wagon rose slowly at the front, showing the shiny inner sleeve of the ram behind the dirty cab. The blocks slid out in a rumbling roar. A cloud of dust rose.

'No! Couldn't you wait till I came!' Hal was shouting.

The driver hung out of his cab. 'All right?'

'They should've been on the road, not buggering up my grass!'

'This fellow showed us where to go.' It was clear he wasn't getting out of his cab. Eddie had moved to sneck the tailgate as the body of the wagon lowered, and Hal looked disgusted with arms akimbo for a while before going to the window of the cab, where the driver's brown forearms centred on a receipt book in which he wrote heavily. He handed it out and Hal signed through the carbon. He was given the top copy and folded it deliberately, putting it in his back pocket.

The lorry was heard changing gear and fading down the road. Their nostrils were full of dust, and the sun's heat was noticeable in the quiet. Eddie turned to Hal.

'Going to mix us a batch?'

'Aye, right!' Hal clapped hands to his clean trousers. 'I'll just . . .'

While he was away Eddie shifted the blocks, six to a barrow load. 'Bastard,' he said, the first time he passed the nest. He trundled till he'd laid out enough for three courses. He rubbed a trowel clear of rust, feeling the thinness of his skin, worn by the blocks, and he mixed a batch, and had started to lay the first course, working out of the barrow. There was Hal in jeans.

Eddie emptied the barrow and nodded. 'And bring a sheet of tin to dump it on, eh?'

Hal wheeled back to the tips.

'Four to one!' Eddie shouted. The first course laid he looked down the line, tapped a block into true and settled down to wait.

Hal brought a full load, dragging the barrow legs on the ground so that it didn't slop over. He straightened and rubbed his back.

Eddie sliced the trowel through the mix. 'Dead on. Keep it coming like that old son. Where's the tin?'

'Hey.'

'Sheet of ply, anything.'

They worked in silence after that, till with the third load Hal said, 'That's all you'll be getting. Cement's run out.'

'Christ.'

'Couple of shovels left.'

'Can't you go for some?'

'The wife's car.' Hal shrugged. 'I'll phone them. We can get on with the rest.'

'Like what?'

'The shed. My work shed.'

He went into the house and soon after Margaret came out with sandwiches and a glass of juice.

'Was your Dad a builder?' she asked as he was eating.

'Riveter – that's till he was put out of work. Just the booze then. I wanted to be like my old man when he was working. After I'd have gone to sea.' They'd been watching a butterfly opening and closing its wings, seemingly a form of sunbathing. He pretended to grab it and it fluttered away. 'I'd go down to the river. Watch the cranes. Ships going down, away round the world. Some of the fellows on deck would wave, but I never took my hands out my pockets. Envied every last one of them.'

The heat was amazing. The bread on the last sandwich curling up and beads of sweat on her lip.

'Will you try for a building job?' She'd begun to walk back and he'd gone with her pushing the barrow. 'Hal's got contacts,' she said.

'Hah!'

She went in before he'd thanked her for the sandwiches. Making a small batch with the last two shovels of cement he thought, bugger his shed. I'll finish this and vamoose.

The second and third courses were finished except for the ends; the wall was two and a half feet high and true; given a whole day he'd have built a whole stretch of wall; smashing, with the trowel, line and level.

'Got a hammer and chisel?' he asked Hal when he came out.

Hal nodded and went up to his shed. He was there some time, probably messing about with the bits and pieces for erecting it, and then he came back swinging a 4 lb hammer. 'No chisel!'

He turned a block on its side. Two medium blows with the edge of the hammer split it, half dropping to the ground, and he plastered the broken face and set it on the end of the wall, tapping it firm with the trowel handle.

'They taught you well, boy.'

He plastered the other half of the block, set it on the opposite end and checked it with the level. There remained

THE FOX'S NEST

only to wash the barrow and trowel and shovels; unless cement was about to arrive. He put the trowel, shovel and hammer in the barrow. He wheeled it to the tap at the house. A minute to wash the things and there'd have to be something to say, and the bastard was silent, knowing and enjoying etc. etc., owning his garden and his house and standing there. To ask for the money! His hands shook, making him fumble the water over the blade of the trowel, but he cleaned it and that was it; he turned to Hal who'd come up behind him, and he seemed to take in breath, an endless drawing-in.

Hal was talking.

'. . . so that's the building for today. Right? Tomorrow morning,' he added, maybe repeating it.

He was to barrow the rest of the blocks to the wall. He suddenly remembered that. A way out: take these down for you then I'm finished, settle up now, and so on . . .

'We'll start putting the shed up,' Hal said.

He was thinking about the straight wall through the lumps of earth and began to feel pretty well okay. Ask for the money at dinner time, he thought, but he forgot it. Actually the thing was crystal clear now, he didn't have to bother thinking.

'Okay, let's start the shed.'

Hal stared when smiled at, then he smiled back and led the way round the house. He'd dragged the boat out of the way and moved the wall sections into position. It seemed to be a case of bolting them together, then hauling up the roof trusses, then the felted roof cladding. He'd even fixed the pulley to the loop of wire round the neighbour's tree, and its lower end hung just over their heads.

'How do you fix the sections to it?'

'Slip-chain we had for the dog. Alsatian,' he added sharply. 'It's a strong chain. Now, the first thing's the sides.'

Eddie had picked up a bit of string. As Hal bent to pick up the bag of bolts he kneed him in the stomach. Hal crumpled and he knelt on him, pulled the wrists behind his back and tied them; dragged him by the feet to below the pulley and tied the feet with the other end of the string. Hal's face was grazed and dusty. He'd made a lunge while being dragged, otherwise had not struggled.

'Where's the dog chain?'

He drew his foot back slowly and let it fall against the ribs showing through the yellow T-shirt . . . Threatened to kick again. Hal was trying to free his hand to point but he didn't speak, nodding towards the toolbag that had been under the boat. The chain was on top, perhaps he had got it ready.

Easy. His heart beating hard, he put the chain over Hal's head and let the end lie on his back in the vee of his arms. Easy.

'Now get up!' He jerked the arms. When Hal rolled and sat up he got behind, heaving him to his feet; slipped his hand into the trouser pocket, caught the handkerchief, folded it and tied a gag. 'Useful, eh? These big hankies?' It made a red gash, white spotted across Hal's jaw, the knot nestling between the bony lumps at the back of his skull. Hal's eye swivelled down to look at him.

'Keep the balance, I'm hooking you up.' He put the ring on the end of the dog chain into the jaws of the pulley block and closed them. Hal was swaying. Eddie steadied him, took close hold and gently positioned him.

The free end of the pulley rope was to hand; he pulled, making it seat in the pulley wheels and take the tension, lifting the chain off the back of Hal's neck. He adjusted the links to lie flat in the angle of the jaw and took the remaining tension. 'Right? Off we go.'

A moo came from the gag, the knees buckled and braced, cords stood out on the neck, the eyes glared.

He tucked the pulley rope into the string round the wrists. 'If you fall . . . eh?'

He was running across the garden. And looking over to the hills. But out of the question.

Margaret was at the sink washing vegetables. 'Lettuce again,' she said.

'Can't get enough of it.' There was a range of kitchen

knives in a holder on the wall and he was taking the small one.

'What are you doing?'

He shook his head vaguely and she followed him out. The million granite chips in the roughcast wall seemed to be directing the sun from their facets straight into his eyes, blurring her freckled collarbones and faded green T-shirt. She walked slowly in the sunshine, walking with a firm roll of the bum, old shoes pacing the gravel, old suedes, old mottled things. They could have been going for a walk the two of them.

There was a thump, the squeak of pulleys, hiss of nylon rope and both of them ran.

Hal lay on his side, the ropes sagging in a curve from the branch to his neck, the free end of rope lying at an angle.

He saw what would have happened if the free end instead of pulling through had jammed in the block: the body would have jerked to a halt before hitting the ground.

They had stopped. But she ran forward again. Looking up at him, and down to loosen the chain, crouching beside Hal, she was scared.

He moved slowly towards them, his arms hanging and the knife in his right hand pointing down. She stared at him till he seemed to walk along a beam joining their eyes. And he held her gaze till he was beside them and lowered himself on to Hal's hip. The steel blade was four inches long. He inserted its point between Hal's wrists and cut the string. Then he pressed on his cheek to make room for the blade and slit the gag. Hal turned his head up. One movement slit the ankle string; he placed the knife on the ground, raised off the hip and squatted.

THE FACE
Brian McCabe

He didn't want to see the face.

It was like a railway tunnel, except this tunnel sloped down the way, down through the dripping darkness, down into the deep, dark ground. He could see the dark shine of the rails and he could feel the ridges of the wooden sleepers through the soles of his gymshoes. It was very dark. He was glad his father was there with him.

It would be good to go back up to the daylight now, where the miners were sitting round a brazier, eating their pieces and drinking hot tea from big tins with wire handles. One of them had given him a piece and let him drink some tea from his tin and had pointed to different birds and told him their names, while the other miners talked about the pit and how it was closing. One of them had said he'd be quite happy never to see the face again.

He remembered the first time he'd heard about it: his father came in late from the pit and walked into the kitchen very slowly and sat down still with his coat on. Then he took off his bunnet and looked at it and put it on the kitchen table and talked to his mother in the quiet voice not like his usual voice. Like he couldn't say what he had to say, like when some of the words get swallowed. Because somebody had got killed at the face, John Ireland had got killed at the face, so he'd had to go to Rosewell to tell his wife. That was why he was late. Then his mother took a hanky from her apron pocket and sat down and started crying, and his father put his hands on her shoulders and kissed her like it was

Christmas except this was a different kind of kiss. Then his father looked up at him and nodded to him to tell him to go through to the other room, so he went through and watched TV and wondered how the face had killed John Ireland, the man who ran the boxing gym for boys, and how something terrible could make people need to kiss each other.

He could hear the water dripping from the roof of the tunnel and trickling down the walls and the scrape and crunch of his father's pit boots on the ground. They sounded too loud, but in the dark you had to hold on to sounds, like when you shut your eyes and pretended to be blind, hold on to them to stop yourself hearing what was behind them, where it was like the darkness was listening.

Every few steps he could see the wooden props against the walls, but they were nearly as dark as the walls. And he could just make out the shapes of the wooden sleepers and the rails, but he didn't like the darkness between the sleepers and between the props. If you looked at darkness like that too long you started seeing things in it: patterns, shapes, faces . . .

He listened to his father's voice. It sounded too loud, and crackly like a fire, but you could hold on to it. He was telling him about the bogeys that used to run up and down on the rails in the old days, taking the coal up to the pithead. It was good to hear his father's voice talking about the old days, but he didn't like the sound of the bogeys. He asked what a bogey was and listened as his father told him it was sort of like a railway carriage on a goods train. He knew that anyway, but he wanted to hear his father telling him again, just in case.

There were other bogeys – bogeymen. He asked if there were bogeymen down the pit. His father laughed and said that there weren't. But he knew different, he knew that it was dark enough down here for bogeymen, especially now the word had been said out loud. Bogeymen.

Sometimes if you said a word over and over again it started to sound different. It started to mean something

THE FACE

else, to mean what it sounded like it meant. Then, if you kept on saying it over and over again, it started to not mean anything, the word started to be a thing. And the thing didn't mean anything except what it was.

He tried it now, saying it under his breath over and over again, bogeymen, bogeymen, bogeymen, bogeymen . . . But before the word could lose its meaning, his father stopped walking. He stopped too and turned, glad that they were going to go back up to the light, to the ordinary world.

'You go on,' said his father.

At first he wondered what his father meant, then he knew: he wanted him to keep on walking down into the dark. Alone. He pretended not to have heard and took a step towards the entrance of the tunnel, then he felt his father's hand on his shoulder and his heart pounding in his chest.

'Down you go,' said his father.

He didn't move. He didn't say anything, hoping his father would lose his patience with him and change his mind.

'Are you feart?' said his father.

'Naw, but . . .'

But what? He turned to the darkness. He could still see the rails and the props and the sleepers, but only just. He didn't want to see the face.

'Go on.'

He started walking down into the darkness. He had sometimes seen it in his dreams, after his father had come home late and spoken in the quiet voice to his mother about John Ireland: at first there was just the dark, the pitch-black dark that was blacker than coal, because even coal wasn't always black, because sometimes it was blue or grey, and sometimes it had a dark shine to it, like the cover of the Bible, and sometimes the coal had seams – of fool's gold, or the thin, brittle, silvery seams of mica – but the darkness in the dream had no shine to it, no seams, it was pure black. Then you felt it there like a shadow in the dark, a shadow that went long and went wide, went thick like a wall and went thin like a thread, then the shadow had the shape of a man and the man had a face and the face was the face of John Ireland.

He stopped walking, turned round and looked back at his father. He called to him and asked if he'd gone far enough.

'Further.'

It was good to hear his father's voice behind him, but it didn't last long enough to hold on to. Why didn't his father walk down further too? Why did he have to walk down on his own? Sometimes his father liked him to walk in front of him along the street. 'Walk in front,' he'd say, 'where I can see you.' Like the time he'd taken him to the gym to see John Ireland and he'd seen John Ireland's face. It looked like a bulldog's with a flattened nose and a crushed ear and big, bloodshot eyes. In the dream it looked worse. In the dream, somehow you forgot it was the face of an old boxer. John Ireland had given him a pair of boxing gloves. He'd tied them together and put them round his neck on the way home. And his father had told him to walk in front where he could see him. But that wasn't the reason, not the real reason he wanted him to walk in front. It was because he wanted to dream about his son being a champion boxer. He hadn't gone back to the gym because his mother had put her foot down, but he still put the gloves on sometimes and pretended to be a champion boxer. Now there wasn't a gym because of what had happened at the face.

Maybe it wouldn't be like the face in his dream, but he still didn't want to see it. He stopped and turned round. He could still see the dark shape of his father against the light from the start of the tunnel. He shouted to him and waited.

'Go on.'

His father's voice faded to an echo.

He turned and walked further down into the dark, the pitch-black dark even blacker than coal, then he felt it there, a shadow in the dark . . . He stopped, turned and shouted to his father. He could still see the dim, greyish light from the start of the tunnel, but now he couldn't see his father. He shouted out again. His own voice echoed and he heard the fear in it, then all there was was the listening darkness all around and the pounding of his heart. The shadow had the shape of a man and the man had a face . . .

THE FACE

As he turned to run away he was lifted in the air and his father's laughter filled his ear. He was laughing and saying he was proud, proud of him because he'd walked down on his own, proud because now he was a man.

He rubbed the bus window with his hand and looked out at the big, black wheel of the pit. He watched it getting smaller as the bus pulled away, till it was out of sight.

'Why are they gonnae shut the pit? Is there nae coal left in it?' he asked.

'There's plenty coal,' said his father, angrily.

'Why then?'

'The government wants it shut.'

'Where'll ye go tae work then?'

'Mibbe in Bilston Glen.'

'Is that another pit?'

'Aye.'

He waited a minute, then he asked, 'Has it got a face as well?'

'Aye, it's got a face.'

'Is it like the face in your pit?'

His father shrugged. 'Much the same.'

'Ah saw it.'

'What?'

'The face.'

His father shook his head and smiled at him, the way he did when he thought he was too young to understand something.

'Ah did see it.'

'Oh ye did, did ye? What did it look like?'

'It looked like the man who ran the gym.'

And he knew he'd said something very important when his father stopped smiling, turned pale, opened his mouth to say something but didn't say anything, then stared and stared at him – as if he couldn't see him at all, but only the face of the dead man.

BIOGRAPHICAL NOTES

FRANK COUTTS is an animal nutritionist, trained at Aberdeen. His other personal details he notes as follows: 'two children; large novel now in nth revision; blushes easily'.

PETER REGENT was born in Suffolk and educated in Norfolk and at Oxford. He has now lived in Fife for more than twenty years. His collection of short stories, *Laughing Pig*, was published by Robin Clark in 1984.

JOHN KERR was born in Hamilton and educated in Glasgow. He worked for British Steel then headed South, when he was made redundant, to attend the National Film School. He is the writer and producer of numerous short stories and short films, including 'The Riveter' broadcast on BBC in September 1988. He currently works as a lawyer in the City.

CHRIS ARTHUR was born and educated in Belfast, but has lived in Scotland since 1974. He has worked as a nature reserve warden, a teacher, a television researcher and is currently employed on the University of Edinburgh's 'Media and Theological Education' project. He was awarded the Akegarasu Hays International Essay Prize in 1986.

SUSAN CHANEY was born in Edinburgh and is now a post-graduate student at Edinburgh University. She has three children, two of whom are twins. This is her first published story.

JENNY TURNER was born in Aberdeen and now lives in Edinburgh. She works part-time as a teacher and in a community centre. She has written many books reviews and essays for a number of publications, but this is her first piece of fiction to be published.

DRUMMOND BONE was born in Ayr in 1947 and educated at Ayr, Glasgow and Oxford. He returned from the South to lecture at Glasgow University in 1980, and now lives in Fife. He has completed two novels and primarily sees himself as a writer rather than an academic.

FRANK KUPPNER was born in Glasgow in 1951. Poet, playwright, critic and serious thinker, his works include: *A Bad Day for the Sung Dynasty* (1984); *The Intelligent Observation of Naked Women* (1987); *Ridiculous! Absurd! Disgusting!* (1989).

KEN ROSS is a freelance writer, born and educated in Edinburgh, now living in London. He has had plays performed at the Gate, Almost Free and Royal Court theatres in London, the Traverse Theatre, Edinburgh, and on Granada Television. His story 'The Wardrobe' appeared in last year's collection of *Scottish Short Stories*.

CAROLE MORIN was born in 1964 in Glasgow, went to school in New York, and now lives in London.

WILLIAM RAEPER was born in Kirkcaldy, Fife in 1959, studied English at Oxford, mime in Paris and theology in Nottingham. He has published a biography of George MacDonald, the nineteenth-century Scottish writer, and a book of short fairy tales for children. He now lives in Oxford where he teaches occasionally and tries to write.

MOIRA BURGESS was born in Campbeltown in 1936. She has published two novels, *The Day Before Tomorrow* (1971) and *A Rumour of Strangers* (1987); edited a collection of Scottish women's writings; co-edited a collection of Glasgow short stories; and compiled *The Glasgow Novel: a bibliography* (2nd edition 1986). Her short stories have appeared in *Scottish Short Stories* 1985 and 1986, and elsewhere. She was awarded Scottish Arts Council bursaries in 1982 and 1987.

JUSTINE CABLE has had a chequered career as a civil servant, newspaper reporter, hippie, anthropologist and computer programmer. In addition to building most of the furniture, she's decorated her family's home in Scotland with paintings and tapestries when she has not been occupied with writing. She has two grown sons.

BIOGRAPHICAL NOTES

TIM NIEL was born in 1962; he studied history at Edinburgh University. His previously published work has appeared in *Clanjamfrie 2* and *New Writing Scotland 5*.

JENNIFER MURRAY was born in Ballater, Aberdeenshire. She worked for several years as a news and arts reporter for BBC television before moving to the theatre as a director and playwright. 'Best Friends' is her first published short story.

JOHN CUNNINGHAM was born in Edinburgh in 1934, and has spent most of his life farming in Galloway. He now lives in Glasgow.

BRIAN MCCABE was born in Edinburgh in 1951. He studied Philosophy and English Literature at Edinburgh University before he was awarded a writer's bursary by the Scottish Arts Council in 1980. Since then, he has worked as a freelance writer; his most recent publications include *The Lipstick Circus* (Mainstream) and *One Atom to Another* (Polygon).

COVER ARTIST: ALISON WATT finished her Post-Graduate Studies at Glasgow School of Art in 1988. During her time at College, she exhibited her work at the Royal Academy, and National Portrait Gallery in London and won several major prizes including the British Institution Fund Prize and the prestigious John Player Portrait Award. 'I am primarily concerned with the direct relationship between the figure and particular inanimate objects. Certain gestures and elements of still-life reoccur drawing attention to the poised awkwardness of the composition, offering unanswered questions to the viewer.' In November 1988, her work was shown with five other women artists at the Scottish Gallery, Edinburgh.